TICKET
TO
LOVE

MARILYN KAYE

TICKET
TO
LOVE

Hodder
Children's
Books

A division of Hachette Children's Books

A Catalogue record for this book is available from the British Library

ISBN 978 1 444 90310 2

Typeset in Berkeley by Avon DataSet Ltd,
Bidford-on-Avon, Warwickshire

Printed and bound by CPI Group
(UK) Ltd, Croydon, CR0 4YY

The paper and board used in this paperback by Hodder Children's Books
are natural reyclable products made from wood grown in
sustainable forests. The manufacturing processes conform to the
environmental regulations of the country of origin.

Hodder Children's Books
a division of Hachette Children's Books
338 Euston Road, London NW1 3BH
An Hachette UK company
www.hachette.co.uk

For Meredith Friedman, who shared with me
an eventful long weekend away.

Chapter One

Megan could hear her mobile ringing as she twisted the key in the lock. Entering her flat, she dropped her shopping and fumbled in her bag for the phone. When she saw the name on the screen she considered letting it go to voicemail. But this was the third call from her mother, and she'd have to take it sooner or later.

'Hello, Mum.'

'Megan, where *are* you?'

Megan pretended not to hear the aggrieved tone. 'Home. In my flat.'

'Perhaps I should have asked, where *were* you?'

She couldn't play dumb for too long. 'Oh, right. I was supposed to come to the shop this afternoon. I'm truly sorry, Mum, but something came up.'

'Something like what?' her mother demanded frostily. 'Did you chip a fingernail?'

Megan ignored the sarcasm. '*No*. I ran into Sophie Connors. You remember Sophie? From ballet.'

'Ballet? That was – what? Six years ago?'

'I know, I'm surprised I even recognised her! But anyway, I did, and we started talking, and she's got all these problems, Mum, you wouldn't believe it. She's madly in love with this guy she met at uni, but he's from this family that believes in arranged marriages, and he's practically engaged to a girl he hasn't even met back in India, and if he disobeys his parents they'll disown him! I absolutely had to sit down with her and listen to the whole story.'

None of this was a lie. The only bit of information she was leaving out was the fact that it had happened a week ago. She simply couldn't give her mother the real excuse for not showing up today.

'I'll come and help out tomorrow, Mum, I swear. And I have to go now, I've got the girls coming over tonight.' She didn't have to explain further – the Thursday evening get-togethers had become almost a religious ritual, and her mother respected that.

'Well, give them all my regards, and I'll expect you at the shop tomorrow . . . You do want this job, don't you, Megan?'

'Of course I do, Mum. See you tomorrow.'

She wasn't so sure that she did actually *want* the job, but she definitely needed it. Especially after today's activities. Her credit card hadn't spent much time inside her wallet. She hadn't actually *planned* to blow off her job and spend the day shopping, but when she'd seen the sign outside one of her absolutely favourite stores, she had no choice. *No one* could be expected to ignore a sale like that!

She carried the bags into the bedroom and dropped them on her bed, but she didn't take out the contents immediately. She wanted to simply enjoy the anticipation of seeing her purchases again. For a moment, she felt like a little girl on Christmas morning, gazing in delight and wonderment at the wrapped packages under the tree. Of course, this was different, in that she knew what she'd find in these bags. But that didn't make it any less exciting.

Slowly, savouring every moment, she began removing each item. A grey cashmere sweater from Ralph Lauren, soft and fine, and it would go perfectly with the Stella McCartney black pencil skirt she'd bought the week before. A pair of ballerina flats in the most adorable shade of mustard yellow. Leopard print patterned leggings, Juicy Couture. Skinny black Superfine jeans.

She consciously saved the best for last. The handbag was wrapped in wads of tissue, and she took her time removing the layers. She held it at arm's length and appreciated the warm, caramel colour, almost exactly the same colour as her hair. She admired the sweet little pockets with the brass clasps, the elegant stitching on the flap, the little bronze disc that proclaimed the bag to be a genuine Mulberry. Then she hugged it, taking in deep breaths of the delicious leather smell. This was the one item that hadn't been on sale, but she couldn't pass it up.

She brought the bag back out into the sitting room and set it beside the telly, so it would be in plain view of her guests. Erica and Serena might not notice it, but Jennifer would instantly recognise the new 'it' bag of the season. And she would demonstrate her appreciation – possibly with a scream of envy.

Then Megan busied herself getting ready for the imminent arrival of her friends, tidying up the room, setting out the nibbles and drinks. When they first began these Thursday evening get-togethers, almost a year earlier, they'd taken turns hosting the event. But ultimately, they all agreed that meeting here was nicer than sprawling on the floor of the bedsit shared by Jen and Serena, or huddling together on the bed in

Erica's room in the apartment above the restaurant. Besides, Megan was the only one with a decent sized, flat screen TV.

As far as accommodation went, she was the luckiest of the four of them, and she knew it. This place certainly wasn't what would be termed a luxury flat, but it was a good size and it was located in a good, central neighbourhood. Her parents had purchased the flat as an investment some years earlier, and when the last tenant had moved out, Megan talked her parents into letting her move in. They weren't getting much return on their investment now – Megan wasn't paying any rent – but they weren't complaining about it. Megan was an only child, and they were happy to know she was living in a safe and comfortable place.

And other than providing her with a free living space, it wasn't as though they had to actually support her. She could thank her grandfather for that. He'd founded the family business, a chain of launderettes, and he'd set up little trust funds for his grandchildren, Megan and her two cousins. It wasn't a princely sum, but it provided for the essentials and gave her the right to own several credit cards. And she hadn't maxed them out – not yet, at least.

Her income would soon be supplemented by the wages she would earn once her mother's shop was up and running. Her mother didn't need to work, but she'd always had a passion for exotic, luxury items for the home, and setting up a small boutique to sell them was her new hobby. Helping out there would make a nice little job for Megan. It wasn't as if her mother would fire her for not showing up every now and then.

There was a buzz from the intercom. Megan hurried into the kitchen and looked at the screen displaying the lobby. Seeing Serena, she hit the button to open the building's door.

Even though Serena wouldn't recognise the importance of Megan's new bag, she couldn't resist having it over her shoulder when she opened the door to the flat.

'Hi, come on in.'

'Am I the first?' Serena asked as she entered.

'Aren't you always?' Megan asked, turning to the side to show off her bag. 'Well, what do you think?

'About what?'

Megan stared at her friend.

'My new bag! I just got it today. Isn't it gorgeous?'

Serena looked nonplussed. 'What happened to your old bag?'

'I've still got it, along with several others. You know, Serena, it's not generally considered bizarre to have more than one handbag. You might want to consider buying a nice new one yourself. How much longer are you going to carry that plastic thing on your back?'

Serena slid her knapsack off. 'It's not plastic, it's something called PVC. And I've never seen a handbag that could carry half a dozen books as comfortably as this does. Along with a giant bottle of Diet Coke.' She removed that last item and handed it to Megan, who put it on the coffee table.

'Thanks,' Megan said, but she hadn't finished offering her fashion advice. 'Seriously, Serena, a tote bag would look much nicer. I've seen some really nice canvas ones, not expensive at all.'

Serena sank into a chair. 'Please, no lectures! I've been listening to lectures all day. The ideal of harmony and balance in the High Renaissance. Hieronymous Bosch and "The Garden of Earthly Delights". Forms of classicism.'

Megan could offer no response to that. As far as *she* was concerned, classicism was a word she would use to describe Louis Vuitton accessories. Serena was the intellectual of the group. She was studying art history at uni, and she took it seriously. Her dream was to become a museum curator. Jennifer was at the uni with her, but for Jen it was mainly a means to meet the right kind of guy – and put off finding a job.

But while Serena might be the smartest, she was totally clueless in other ways. OK, she was a student and she didn't have a ton of money, but that didn't mean she had to walk around looking like a homeless waif. The baggy, shapeless trousers, the faded jumper, the worn-out Converse trainers – there was no excuse to look like that, not when there was Zara and H&M and other stores that could give a girl an up-to-date look for reasonable prices. And that hair! A few well-placed streaks could brighten up that mousy brown mop, and a little make-up would do wonders. For years, Megan and Jen had tried to steer Serena in the direction of a makeover, but to no avail. How could a girl be so smart and so ignorant at the same time?

Megan gave up for the time being. 'Where's Jen?'

'I don't know,' Serena said. 'I haven't seen her since breakfast.'

Megan frowned. It was almost time, and Jennifer was never late. She adored this TV show. Of all of them, she was the biggest fan. A buzzing from the kitchen sent Megan back to the intercom. 'Maybe that's her now.'

Moments later, Jennifer hurried into the flat.

Megan regarded her curiously. 'What's the matter . . . you look all agitated?'

Jennifer was pushing off her coat, revealing a typically

slinky dress and six-inch designer heels. 'Is everyone here yet?' she said in response. 'I've got amazing news that concerns all of us!'

Megan and Serena exchanged a look.

'What news?' said Megan. 'The last time I saw you this excited was the day you accidentally spilt your coffee over Sienna Miller in Notting Hill Starbucks!'

Jennifer laughed, throwing her coat over the back of Megan's sofa. 'This is way better than that. Is Erica here yet?'

Serena shook her head. 'She must have got held up at the restaurant.'

'Let's wait for her before I tell you.' Jennifer helped herself to a Diet Coke from Megan's fridge. 'I promise . . . it's worth waiting for . . .'

Chapter Two

It was almost eight o'clock on this unusually warm Thursday evening, and while the sun was setting in a brilliantly clear September sky, and the rest of the world was relaxing at home at the end of the working day – or out enjoying the glorious weather – Erica Douglas was chopping onions. Which had to be her least favourite task in the world.

She didn't much like peeling carrots or scrubbing potatoes either, but chopping onions was the worst. Not only was it a monotonous activity, but she couldn't even use the monotony to daydream for fear of slicing off a finger or two with the small, ultra-sharp knife.

Catching a glimpse of herself in the metal panel that faced her work station, she knew the reflection was distorted, but that couldn't conceal how truly awful she looked. Her face had lost any trace of the make-up she'd applied in the morning. An ugly pink net covered her head, mashing her curls and clashing horribly with their dark red colour. Beads of sweat dotted her forehead, and the top of her apron was covered with evidence of the food she'd been chopping, slicing, dicing and peeling. And there were tears running down her cheeks. The tears were caused by the onions, she knew that, but they might just as well have been brought on by the sorry state of her life.

Another image entered the reflection.

'You OK, Erica?'

She managed a wan smile for the gangly boy hovering over her, and wracked her brain for the new employee's name.

'I'm fine, Harry. It's just the onions.'

'Oh, OK. Um, Erica . . . what time do you get off?'

'Eight-thirty.'

'Yeah? Me too! Want to go out and get something to eat?'

She answered kindly but truthfully. 'I'm sorry, Harry, I've got plans.'

'Oh, OK,' he said again, blushing. 'Another time?'

'Sure,' she lied. Harry was a nice boy, but he couldn't be more than sixteen or seventeen, at least two years younger than she was. And after eight hours in a

11

restaurant kitchen, the last thing on her mind was going to another restaurant. Not to mention the fact that Harry wasn't very attractive and right now he smelled like the fish he'd been cleaning.

Thinking of smells, she had a feeling that an hour of chopping onions meant she must be putting out some pretty nasty odours herself. She glanced at the big clock on the wall. If she could finish work fifteen minutes early, she'd have enough time to go upstairs, shower and change before heading out for the evening.

Her boss had just entered the kitchen. Wiping her hands on her apron, she hurried over to the heavy-set but nicely dressed man. He looked harried, but she plunged in anyway.

'Uncle Tony, I was wondering . . .'

'Not now, sweetheart, it's insane out there, I've got a party of ten and they all want the special.' His voice rose as he addressed the head chef. 'How are we doing on meat sauce?'

'Running low,' the chef yelled back. 'I got meat browning but I need more veg.'

Erica sighed. The special was spaghetti bolognaise, so 'veg' meant onions and peppers, finely chopped. 'I'll get back to work,' she murmured.

Her uncle rubbed the worry lines on his forehead and

looked apologetically at her. 'Did you want to ask me something, Erica?' he said more kindly.

She hesitated. She could claim a sudden massive headache. Uncle Tony could always corral some poor waiter into coming back here and chopping. But that would only make things crazier front of house. She wouldn't do that to him.

'It's nothing, Uncle Tony,' she mumbled, and went back to her station. She wasn't all that desperate, and she could do a quick scrub-up in the restaurant bathroom. She certainly didn't want to add to her poor uncle's aggravation.

After chopping for another ten minutes, the mound of onions had grown appreciably. She emptied them into a bowl and carried them over to the chef.

'Enough?' she asked.

'Give me a dozen more,' he ordered.

It was already eight-thirty. She dashed back to her place and started chopping frantically at twice the normal speed. Annie, the ancient pastry chef, ambled by and smiled at her sympathetically.

'Hot date tonight?' she asked.

Erica shook her head. 'I'm meeting some friends. We get together almost every Thursday night.'

The older woman sighed wistfully. 'I remember those

days. Pub-crawling, hitting the clubs, flirting with strangers . . .'

'Actually, we're just going to watch a TV show.'

Annie's face fell. 'You're kidding! At your age?'

Erica grinned. 'It's a ritual. We hang out, we eat, we watch *Babes in Manhattan*, and we talk.'

'I guess that could be fun,' Annie said doubtfully.

'It is,' Erica assured her. She didn't add that it was the social high point of her week.

Erica watched as the pastry chef moved on, and tried to imagine Annie at her own age. What had been her hopes and dreams back then? Surely not to spend her life stuffing cannoli pastry shells with sweet ricotta cream. She shuddered. Would *she* still be chopping onions forty years from now? Sadly, it was possible. *This* certainly wasn't where she thought she'd be just eighteen months ago.

When Uncle Tony first proposed that she come to work at his restaurant it seemed like a brilliant idea. First off, she'd always been interested in food, and not just eating it. As a small child, when her mother had things to do outside the home, she would drop Erica off at the restaurant to be watched over by her aunt and uncle. But it was Erica who really did the watching. The chopping, mixing, plating and serving – it all seemed like great fun to her. Later, when she was older, she frequently stopped by after school with her friends, and Uncle Tony or Aunt Marie would offer them treats like cannoli and crunchy Italian cookies sprinkled with powdered sugar.

By the time she was thirteen, Erica realised she was becoming more and more intrigued by cuisine in general. While other kids went to bed clutching their copies of a Harry Potter novel, she preferred to curl up with recipe books. While her friends were glued to the latest teen drama or reality show on TV, she was addicted to cookery programmes and competitions. She'd watch them whipping up soufflés, creating delicate sauces, and dream of becoming a chef herself.

There was another reason she liked hanging out at La Trattoria when she was younger. Even between meal services, there was a lively, cheerful atmosphere. Her older cousins, the son and daughter of her aunt and uncle, had both left school and were working there too. They were warm and good-natured, and they made Erica feel like a special kid sister. She was part of the family.

She didn't have this feeling at home. With no siblings to play and squabble with, she'd been a lonely child. As for her parents, they weren't neglectful or anything like that, but they didn't provide much in the way of affection or even companionship. Nor for her, and not for each other either. Even as a very young child, she sensed that her parents weren't in love. They didn't even seem to like each other. Erica's memories of life at home brought her no joy. Mainly, she remembered silence, and an aura of gloom. Her parents were like two ghosts who occasionally drifted through the rooms. La Tratorria became her refuge.

Years later, she learned that her parents had never wanted to be together. Erica had been an accident that forced them to marry. By the time she was fifteen, they'd divorced, which changed the atmosphere at home slightly. Now there was only her mother, one ghost drifting through the rooms instead of two.

Then her mother met a man, and Erica didn't want to be in the way of her mum's chances for a new and happier life. So she moved in with her father, who was living just outside town. He'd remarried, and his wife was pleasant to Erica, but she still felt like she didn't belong there. Her life wasn't terrible, but there wasn't much to be happy about either. At least she had Nate.

A friend since primary school, Nate and Erica had always been very close. Over the years, their relationship had evolved, and by the time they were both fifteen they considered themselves to be boyfriend and girlfriend. It was an easy relationship, comfortable and with very few demands or expectations.

But had she ever really loved Nate in *that* way, or was he just another refuge, like the restaurant? She couldn't say, and it didn't really matter any more. Nate was long gone. The September after they finished school, he left for university. At first, they'd emailed every day, and he'd come home frequently for weekends. Then he became more caught up in life at uni, his circle of friends expanded and Erica suspected that among these friends was a special girl. She knew it was over between them long before he told her.

She couldn't say her heart had been broken. She hadn't cried over Nate. It was just one of those things, and she didn't even find herself thinking about him any more. If she ever had. Besides, she had other things on her mind by then. She'd decided to become a chef.

Her family didn't have the kind of money to send her to one of those fancy culinary institutes, but that didn't really matter. She'd done some research and found that many fine chefs were self-taught, learning their craft as apprentices in restaurants. So Uncle Tony's offer had been quickly accepted.

By then, her cousins had married and left town. Uncle Tony and Aunt Marie offered her a rent-free room in their spacious apartment above the restaurant.

She'd been dying to get away from her father's dreary suburban house. Mum had moved to Spain with her new boyfriend, and Erica had no desire to join them. Now she could live in town and kick off her career. How perfect was that?

Her cousins hadn't been interested in the restaurant business, so her aunt and uncle were very happy to have a family member involved in La Trattoria, and they immediately made plans for her. From the moment she entered their lives, her future was ordained. La Trattoria was her destiny. But as grateful as she was to her aunt and uncle, she couldn't get too excited about this.

La Trattoria was a decent restaurant, the kind that had won loyal patrons. People could count on La Trattoria, they knew what they were going to get. The menu hadn't changed in twenty-five years, nor had the management or the chef. Erica had given up on asking her uncle to introduce new dishes. Even if and when he retired and turned the restaurant over to Erica, he'd be watching her. And it would break his heart if she went so far as to add an extra garlic clove to a dish. After a few months, she realised she was not on the road to a brilliant career as a chef. This was a dead-end job, and she was stuck with it.

She finished chopping the extra onions and raced

18

them over to the chef. He gave her a quick nod, which meant she was dismissed. In the bathroom, she whipped off her apron, pulled the net from her hair and washed her hands. She made a half-hearted and essentially futile attempt to revive her crushed red curls, swiped a slick of gloss across her lips and sprayed herself profusely with a citrus-scented cologne in the hope that it would mask any lingering traces of onion.

Outside the restaurant, she caught her first lucky break of the day – a bus was just coming along and it wasn't packed. She even managed to find a seat, and gratefully sank into it.

The bus had hardly started moving again, however, before there was an ominous sputtering sound and it ground to a halt.

There was a collective groan from everyone on board.

'Sorry folks!' yelled the driver. 'Looks like engine trouble. We might be delayed for a few minutes.'

Erica sighed. A moment of self-pity swept over her. What a sad little life, when a seat on a bus was the best thing that had happened to her all day. But the potential of another spirit-lifter lay in her handbag, and she could take advantage of it right now. She retrieved her mobile phone and touched the icon that would lead her to Friendspace.

This new social network hadn't yet achieved the popularity of Myspace or Facebook, but it was Erica's personal favourite. When you signed up, you entered key words that would give you potential connections. The words could be the names of sports you liked, hobbies, religion, politics, types of music, celebrities – anything you were interested in. The network then gave you the names and photos of other people around the world who had entered some or all of the same keywords. All Erica had entered was beaches, food and a certain Swedish pop group from the 70s. She wanted to keep her options open.

It wasn't a dating service, but Erica had taken advantage of the photos to identify interesting people of the male persuasion. Recalling Annie's remark about a possible 'hot date', she grimaced. She could barely remember the last time she'd had any kind of date at all, let alone a hot one. She supposed she could make more effort to meet some guys right here in town, but it was so much easier, so much *safer*, to meet guys online who she wouldn't have to impress in person.

She now had three interesting relationships on Friendspace. There was Paul, in Australia. He was a surfer – she'd hooked up with him because 'beaches' had been one of his keywords too. His photos revealed an utterly gorgeous boy – tanned and blond – and his tales of riding waves in the Sydney sunshine inspired pleasant fantasies.

Then there was Ronnie in South Africa, who was also a fan of Abba.

But her absolute favourite was Danny, in New York City. He wasn't as drop-dead handsome as Paul, but his looks were appealing – deep-set brown eyes, brown tousled hair. She liked this – guys who looked too 'groomed' had never interested her much. She preferred the more relaxed, casual type. In his photo, Danny wore a T-shirt – she couldn't make out the logo on the front, but the picture of the tree made her suspect it was making some sort of ecological statement. She liked that too.

Their common interest was 'food', though it was just a hobby for him. At only nineteen, he was practically a tycoon; a junior Donald Trump/Richard Branson-type, but with a heart. He came from a background similar to hers, without much money, and he wasn't any better educated than she was, but he was making it on his own. Yet for all his financial success he was totally down-to-earth, and their conversations had revealed they had more in common than the keywords they'd entered. They were both essentially loners, with only a few close friends, and neither was close to their families. Of course, there were big differences too. He was realising his dreams, big time. She was stalled, and her dreams were on hold.

But he didn't write a lot about his career, so she didn't have to converse about hers either. They rarely brought up the day-to-day events of their working days. They talked about current affairs, they recommended books to each other. They compared the cultural differences between the US and the UK. With her other Friendspace correspondents, she sometimes had to struggle to come up with something halfway interesting to report. With Danny, she had no problem at all. Music, hobbies, food, politics, silly TV shows – any subject was open for discussion.

They didn't agree on everything, and they didn't share all their interests. He loved American football, which she found too violent. He thought English football, which he called soccer, was boring. She liked romantic comedies, he liked action films. He really disliked today's popular music, and couldn't understand the appeal of Lady Gaga or Katy Perry, two of Erica's favourite singers. He preferred old, nostalgic music – like the Kinks – and contemporary alternative rock, which Erica thought was boring noise that you couldn't dance to. Danny said he hated to dance.

Usually, they just posted messages to each other, but every now and then, when they were both on Friendspace at the same time, they could have live chats. You couldn't save the chats, but there were some conversations that she could practically recite from memory.

Erica: If you could take a vacation anywhere in the world, where would you go?

Danny: Costa Rica.

Erica: Really? What's special about Costa Rica?

Danny: It's a bird-watcher's paradise.

Erica: You like birds, huh?

Danny: Totally. I've been into bird-watching since I was a kid. Are you interested in birds?

Erica: LOL. No, seriously, not very much. Not at all, actually. Have you ever seen that old movie where the birds go crazy and start attacking people?

Danny: Alfred Hitchcock, The Birds. *Great movie!*

Erica: Maybe so, but ever since I saw it, birds make my skin crawl. Sorry.

Danny: Don't apologise. It's just one more thing we don't have in common!

Erica: If we both joined an online dating service, we'd never be matched.

Danny: That's why I'm glad we met here. I don't

understand those services. Why do people think that just because they have a lot in common, they'll fall in love?

Erica: I agree. Just because two people like the same music or sports, that doesn't mean they'll like each other.

Danny: Absolutely. What makes people fall in love? It's chemistry. Or maybe magic is a better word. Because you can't really explain it.

At that point, she'd wanted to write something like 'This is magic, isn't it?' But she'd restrained herself. It was just too soon for that.

She wished she could hear his voice. He hadn't mentioned having a phone conversation yet, and she couldn't bring it up. It would be too expensive. And Skype was out, since she'd broken her laptop that had the webcam.

In today's message, Danny told her about a restaurant where he'd had dinner the evening before. From his description, Erica could tell it was pretty ritzy, a 'see-and-be-seen' kind of place, with a menu that featured fine wines and 'nouvelle cuisine'. Definitely not a La Trattoria-type joint. He reported seeing a couple of celebrities who overindulged in cocktails, and his depiction of their behaviour made her laugh out loud. The woman in the seat next to her looked alarmed.

'Good news,' the bus driver called out. 'Looks like the

problem's fixed and we're ready to continue our journey.'

Erica checked her watch. The show was nearly over. The others weren't going to be happy with her. Still, it wasn't her fault the bus had broken down. She put her phone back in her bag and stared out of the bus window as it sped closer to Megan's flat. She would read the rest of Danny's story later, happy in the knowledge that it would wait there for her, right in her bag. The smartphone with its Wi-Fi and 3G internet access had been expensive, she couldn't really afford it, but it was worth it to make her feel like Danny was with her, wherever she was.

Chapter Three

Babes in Manhattan was an American series that had become hugely popular in the UK, and Serena could understand why. The tales of four twenty-something single girls in New York City were cleverly written, funny, occasionally touching and always entertaining.

Each of the four main characters had a distinctive and unique personality. There was Kelsey, a gentle soul, mild-mannered and easy-going. She was the most 'centred' of the girls, the one who had her feet planted firmly on the ground. She was devoted to her friends, her job – she was a primary school teacher – and her long-term boyfriend, Jason. Jane was the ultimate career girl, aggressive and ambitious. She worked in a high-powered corporate world where she was constantly struggling to rise, and this frequently got in the way of her love life. Tori was a wealthy, high-society type and something of a snob. Marina was the wild child, a glamorous, sexy party girl who hobnobbed with celebrities and hopped from lover to lover without a thought for the future.

They were all gorgeous, charismatic and popular. They wore fabulous clothes and they went out constantly, to clubs, bars, trendy restaurants. They shopped, they went on vacations to exotic places and there was always a romantic adventure going on. Serena felt reasonably sure the average twenty-something single girl didn't live like this, not even in New York. It was all pretty silly, actually. But of course, the show wasn't supposed to be realistic. There were no vampires or paranormal activities, but *Babes in Manhattan* was still fantasy, pure and simple. Viewers appreciated stories like this as an escape from mundane real life, and liked to live vicariously through the characters.

Serena could understand why her friends needed this show. Jennifer craved glamour, which played no part in her own life, so she idolised Marina. Erica dreamed of having an exciting career, so Jane was her favourite character. Megan was into all the fine things money could buy, so she related to Tori.

Which left Kelsey for Serena. Serena didn't mind, she liked to think of herself as a down-to-earth and generally nice person. The fashion and glamour didn't particularly interest her, and she couldn't connect at all with the way the other girls hopped from man to man. She could see herself, like Kelsey, as a one-man woman – if she could ever find that man.

Relationships with the opposite sex had never come easily to Serena. Sure, she'd had her crushes, her infatuations, but they never seemed to develop into anything. Friends told her she didn't flirt properly, that she never made any effort to appeal to guys. They'd tried to upgrade her style, to tutor her in the ways of attracting a man. She heard them, she pretended to listen to them and she knew they meant well, but she never took their advice to heart. Mainly because she had no interest in changing. Which meant she would probably never find that boy-of-her-dreams. By now, she had pretty much reconciled herself to a life alone.

Tonight's episode centred on Kelsey, who enjoyed her job, but her dream in life was to get married and raise a family. Kelsey had been convinced that she and Jason were heading in that direction. But recently Jason had decided he didn't want to make the big commitment, and he'd ended the relationship. Personally, Serena was sure he'd get back with Kelsey, mostly because the actor who portrayed Jason was incredibly popular and she doubted the makers of the show would want him to disappear permanently from the screen.

But in the current episode, Kelsey was sworn off men and she'd made her own commitment – to give up on her dream and to live alone forever. Another reason why Serena could relate to her. Of course, Kelsey's three best friends were united and determined to bring her out of what they perceived as a tragic state, and each had a different man they wanted to hook her up with. Jane had arranged a date for Kelsey with a guy from her office. Tori had earmarked an upper-crust but intellectually-challenged cousin for her.

In tonight's episode they watched wild-and-crazy Marina push a celebrity playboy in Kelsey's direction. The devastatingly handsome man had no interest in marriage or any sort of permanent relationship, but Marina believed he could show Kelsey a good time until the man of her dreams appeared. Kelsey wasn't particularly interested in the playboy, just as she hadn't been interested in the men Jane and Tori had proposed. But to pacify her friends and to avoid arguments, she was going along with their schemes. Serena predicted that tonight's meeting would be humorously disastrous, just as the others had been. Megan and Jennifer didn't care. They were paying more attention to other aspects of the show.

'I totally love those shoes!' Megan cried out. 'They have to be Manolos.'

'Ooh, they look like six months' salary to me,' Jennifer said admiringly. 'I don't like Kelsey's hair like that. No one over the age of twelve should wear plaits.'

'Oh, I think they're cute!' Megan argued. 'Kelsey can carry off anything.'

Serena hadn't even noticed the shoes, or the controversial hair style. Funny how different they were, she and her three closest friends. Like the 'Babes' on TV, they didn't have much in common. The show had never explored how the characters actually came together in the first place, but Serena could imagine the writers coming up with a background not too unlike the way the four real-life friends had met.

At the age of twelve, they'd all been members of the same Girl Guides unit, and all of them had hated it. Serena didn't like the emphasis on sports, Jennifer found it all too regimented and proper. Erica wasn't into team activities and Megan loathed the unfashionable neckerchiefs they were forced to wear. It had been during one particularly tedious activity that the girls had found themselves moaning to each other in a rainy field somewhere in rural England, and a bond was formed.

Long after Girl Guides was finished, the relationship continued. The girls attended different schools, but they stayed in touch. Now, thanks to their shared enthusiasm for *Babes in Manhattan*, they were getting together weekly. And despite their different personalities, they had become even closer. Personally, Serena believed the show was just an excuse – it was the true affection between the friends that made them want to meet up frequently. Although they'd never admit it, she suspected her friends felt the same way. Except for Jennifer, maybe. *She* was the one who was truly passionate about *Babes in Manhattan*.

'I wish Erica would hurry up and get here,' said Megan, looking at her watch for the twentieth time that evening. 'She's never this late . . . And I can't wait much longer to hear Jen's news!'

Serena rolled her eyes. Trust Megan to have her priorities right.

Suddenly, there was an urgent knocking sound. Megan leaped up and ran to the door.

'Erica, where have you been?' she demanded. 'And how did you get through the doors downstairs without being buzzed?'

'Someone was coming out,' Erica said. 'And I was in a rush. I ran from the bus stop, am I late?'

Megan shrugged. 'It just finished.'

'Oh, shoot.' Erica sighed. 'I need to check something. I just got a text from my aunt.' Erica plopped down into a chair, greeted Serena and pulled out her mobile.

Serena looked at her curiously. 'Since when did your Aunt Marie get into texting?' Erica didn't answer. She seemed totally absorbed in whatever she was reading on the mobile screen. Then a shrill beep told Megan that *she* had a text message.

She picked up her phone and looked at the screen. 'Damn.'

'What's the problem?' Serena asked.

'It's from Luke.'

'And you're saying "damn"? Has the red-hot romance cooled down already?'

'No, no, everything's fine,' Megan murmured as she read the message. 'He wants me to meet him at a pub near his office.'

'So, go,' Serena said.

'Are you crazy?' Megan asked. 'Do you think I'd blow off my best mates for Luke?' Hastily, she tapped out a response. 'Busy, sorry, talk later.' Maybe, someday, she'd meet a guy for whom she'd pass up her friends. But that guy wasn't Luke.

Not that there was anything wrong with him, as a

boyfriend-of-the-moment. He was good-looking, he came from a good family, he had a good future in the bank where he worked. And maybe she should be feeling a tiny bit of remorse that she was putting him off the way she was doing now and had done several times before. But somehow she couldn't drum up any real regret.

She turned to Erica. 'It was a great episode.'

'Sorry.' Erica smiled apologetically.

'What does your aunt want anyway? Is there a problem at the restaurant?' Megan asked her.

'It's nothing,' Erica said quickly, and put her phone back in her bag. 'And I really am sorry to mess up the evening . . .'

Jennifer danced up behind Megan. 'Oh well. Who cares if you did?'

Serena was stunned. '*Who cares?*' she repeated. 'Jennifer, are you feeling all right?'

Jennifer beamed at them. 'Yeah, I mean . . . Erica doesn't need to watch *Babes in Manhattan* when she can *be* a babe in Manhattan – like the rest of us!'

'What are you talking about?' Megan, Serena and Erica asked all at once.

Jennifer's smile grew even wider. 'We won.'

Chapter Four

Megan stared at her friend blankly. Glancing back at Serena and Erica, she saw the same reaction on their faces.

Jennifer was clearly misinterpreting the silence that greeted her announcement. She beamed proudly. 'You're stunned, right? I don't blame you, so was I. Pretty amazing, huh?'

Megan frowned. 'Jennifer, I'll ask you again, *what* are you talking about?'

'We won the contest!' Jennifer exclaimed.

'What contest?'

'Are you having a laugh?' Her eyes swept the room, as she finally realised that no one knew what she was talking about. 'Don't tell me you forgot about it?'

'Forgot about *what*?' Serena asked.

'I told you months ago! I entered us into the *Babes in*

Manhattan competition. How could you not remember? They were advertising it after every episode! And I got the news today. We won!'

Megan dimly recalled the advertisements, and she recalled Jennifer babbling about it. But Jennifer was always dreaming out loud and going on and on about far-fetched notions. No one took her seriously. But it seemed that, for once, Jennifer had actually realised one of her fantasies. And as the impact of her words hit, Megan's mouth fell open and Erica gasped.

Jennifer had their full attention now. Dramatically, she began to read aloud from the email print-out in her hand.

'Corona Productions are pleased to inform you that you have been selected at random as the very first winner of "Be a Babe in Manhattan". You lucky girls are the recipients of four round-trip tickets to New York City, where you will have a grand suite for three nights at Manhattan's famed four-star Palladium, the luxury hotel featured in many episodes of *Babes in Manhatten*, where you will join the stars of our show to celebrate your arrival with their signature peach martini cocktail.'

She must have caught the scepticism on Megan's face. 'It's not a hoax,' she insisted. 'I had to call the production offices in New York to confirm. We can pick any weekend over the next six weeks, and they'll take care of everything. This is for real, you guys! We're going to New York!'

Finally, Jennifer got the response her news deserved. The room erupted in cries of excitement. Erica let out an earth-shattering shriek, and even the usually reserved Serena was hugging herself and hopping up and down.

Megan was totally overwhelmed. 'I can't believe it! This, this is . . . unbelievable!'

'Believe it!' Jennifer said. 'Why are you so surprised? I followed all the rules, I got the entry in on time. I even remembered to put international postage on the envelope.'

Megan rolled her eyes. 'But I'm guessing millions of people did that. Only *you* would enter a contest like this and actually believe you might win.'

'Well, I did, didn't I? Now, let's talk about dates. How about two weeks from now? Erica, can you get off work?'

'I haven't taken a weekend off in six months, my uncle owes me big time.' Erica was fiddling with her phone as she spoke. 'Damn, I don't have any battery left. Megan, can I use your laptop? I need to send an email.'

'Sure, it's in my bedroom,' Megan murmured. She was looking at the calendar hanging in the kitchen alcove. 'I'm supposed to work in my mother's shop that weekend, but I can get out of it. Serena, what about you?'

Serena examined her datebook worriedly. 'I've got a class on Friday mornings.'

'Serena never cuts classes,' Jennifer told Megan.

'Well, it's time to start,' Megan said briskly.

'Yeah, I guess I could miss one session,' Serena said. 'The professor will understand. I mean, how could I pass up an opportunity to visit the Metropolitan Museum of Art?'

Jennifer made a face. 'Honestly, Serena, how can you even think about dusty old museums at a time like this? What about you, Megan? You wouldn't waste your New York time in a museum, would you?'

Megan considered this. 'Some museums have great shops,' she noted. And she recalled articles she'd read about New York shopping. 'Did you know there's a store that stocks over a hundred styles of jeans? And there's a shoe shop that carries last year's Manolo Blahniks for fifty per cent off! Oh, girls, I'm going to shop till I drop!' Then she drew in her breath sharply as she remembered something. 'There's a website that lists all the best shopping in New York. I'm going to print it out right now before I forget.'

She hurried into her bedroom, where Erica was

sitting at the desk in front of the laptop. 'Are you almost finished?'

Erica didn't seem to have heard her. Her eyes were glued to the screen. Megan moved behind her and looked over her shoulder.

The screen showed an online conversation between Erica and someone called Danny.

Erica: I know u r very busy, but I hope we can have time together.

Danny: I can rearrange my schedule for u. I want to show u NYC.

Erica: Can't believe we'll finally meet!

Danny: I can't wait!

'Who's Danny?' Megan asked.

Startled, Erica looked over her shoulder and gave Megan a sheepish look. 'Long story.'

'I want to hear it,' Megan stated. '*Now*.' She called out to the others. 'Hey, girls, Erica has a man in New York!'

Serena and Jennifer ran into the room. Erica groaned.

'OK, OK,' she muttered. Quickly, she typed '*BFN*'.

Serena squinted at the screen. '*BFN*?'

'It means bye for now.' Erica logged off and turned to the others. 'We met on Friendspace. His name's Danny, he's an entrepreneur, he does investments and stuff like

38

that. We talk online every day and . . . and I really like him. More than like.'

Megan was stunned. 'You haven't even mentioned him before!'

'Yeah! Why didn't you tell us about this?' Serena wanted to know.

Erica shrugged and gave them an abashed smile. 'I guess I felt a little embarrassed. I mean, it's so lame, having an online relationship.'

'Are you kidding?' Jennifer exclaimed excitedly. 'My cousin met her husband online!'

Erica smiled dreamily. 'We've been "talking" like this for months. I think I know more about him than I've known about any guy I've actually dated. He's incredible! He's, like, unbelievably successful for his age, he's only nineteen and he's already practically a millionaire. But he's so down to earth! And we've got so much in common, we have the same sense of humour, we understand each other! I feel more comfortable with him than I've ever felt with any boy.'

'Ohmigod,' Megan said, raising an eyebrow. 'You've got it bad.'

Erica nodded happily. 'And now we're going to meet in person. Guys, I'm so excited!'

'But he's a total stranger,' Serena insisted worriedly.

'You have to be careful, Erica.'

'Well, I think this is absolutely thrilling,' Jennifer declared. 'It's like something that would happen on *Babes in Manhattan*!' She hugged herself in glee. 'We are going to have the most fabulous time in New York! We're going to hit all the coolest places. We'll dance, we'll drink peach martinis, we'll fall in love!'

'Calm down, Jen. We're only there for a weekend,' Megan reminded her.

'A *long* weekend,' Jennifer corrected her. 'And we're going to make the most of every thrilling minute.'

It wasn't until Megan went to bed that she realised she'd forgotten to show Jennifer her new handbag. It didn't seem to matter any more though, she thought sleepily. In two weeks she'd be in Handbag Heaven.

Chapter Five

Jennifer had planned to sleep during the flight, mainly so she wouldn't have to waste time doing that once they were in New York. But squeezed into a middle seat between a fat man who snored loudly and a woman with a screaming baby, sleep was not an option.

The girls hadn't been able to get seats together, which was annoying. Even when Jennifer told the airline that they were the guests of a major TV show, it made no difference; all four were placed far apart on the plane. What was even more disappointing to Jennifer was the fact that they'd been seated in economy class. Surely, the real Manhattan babes would be flying in first class, or at least business.

Well, no matter, she thought, and comforted herself with the certain knowledge that she'd be flying first class one of these days, hopefully very soon. And it was her firm conviction that this trip to New York City would provide the opportunity to kick-start this new lifestyle.

Serena was always saying that *Babes in Manhattan* was a fantasy, that no one really lived like those characters. Jennifer didn't agree. She knew the show was fiction and the 'Babes' were characters, but she also knew that there were plenty of real people who led lives like those portrayed on the screen. She saw proof of that in the magazines she read religiously.

One of those magazines was sitting in the pocket of the seat in front of her now, and she took it out. Right there, on the cover, were two highly recognisable figures – a certain top model and Leonardo Di Caprio. They'd been snapped while coming out of a restaurant in – where else? – New York City, of course. Flipping through the magazine, she spotted at least a dozen other celebrities caught on camera in New York: at a fashion show, entering a hotel, leaving a Broadway theatre, strolling through Central Park. A rock star at Bungalow 8, the hot club. A famous socialite at Tiffany's, the jewellery store.

This was definitely the city where one could find celebrities. Of course, Los Angeles was that kind of city too, but Los Angeles was supposed to be vast and spread out, and everyone went around in cars. It would be much easier to spot celebrities in New York, where people actually walked on the streets. These were the people who lived like the 'Babes', who flew first class, who enjoyed the best of everything. These people didn't live in shabby bedsits, they didn't go to boring classes every day. They didn't eat in fast-food restaurants or hang out in ordinary neighbourhood pubs. Their lives were filled with luxury and glamour, and Jennifer planned to experience a life like that this weekend.

Despite what her friends thought, Jennifer believed she was a realistic person. She knew she could never become a celebrity herself. She had no particular talent that might lead her to fame and fortune. She couldn't sing or act, and she wasn't tall enough to be a model. But you didn't have to be a celebrity to live like one. If she could find a celebrity lover, or even just a celebrity friend, this could be the key to the life of her dreams. And while Erica hung out with her online boyfriend, Megan shopped, and Serena went to museums, Jennifer planned to spend her weekend looking for this key to her future.

She leaned back in her seat, closed her eyes and began to visualise. She'd seen a film once, a true film, that proposed a sure-fire means of getting everything you wanted in life through visualisation. The idea was that if you could see it happening in your mind, if you concentrated and believed that something was possible, it would send out the right vibes and what you wanted would come to you.

She concentrated on the immediate future. According to the prize announcement, when they arrived at the hotel they would meet the stars of the TV show and party with them. She saw herself chatting with the actress who played Marina, laughing and bonding with her. The actress would then invite her to a party at her luxurious penthouse, where she'd be surrounded by exciting people. There would be invitations to dinners, VIP rooms at clubs, more parties. At some point during all these events, she'd meet a man who would fall madly in love with her and beg her not to leave New York. And she'd say goodbye to shabby bedsits and boring classes for ever.

She was visualising so hard that she didn't even hear the pilot's announcement. It wasn't until a flight attendant ordered her to fasten her seatbelt that she realised they were about to land.

Then it was all standing in line and waiting to get off the plane, standing and waiting for a bus to the terminal, more standing and waiting to get her passport stamped. Finally, she arrived at baggage reclaim where she found her friends.

'What time is it?' Serena asked.

Megan had already adjusted her watch. 'Seven-twenty,' she announced.

Serena yawned. 'Which means it's after midnight our time. I'm ready for bed.'

'Bed?' Jennifer shrieked. 'Are you crazy? We're in New York! And we're meeting the Babes in one hour! Serena, pull yourself together.'

'OK, OK,' Serena murmured. She yawned again and rubbed her eyes. Jennifer gazed at her friend and flatmate with a mixture of exasperation and affection. Serena was so sweet, so thoughtful, so generous – and so totally out-of-it. She would need her friends to look after her this weekend if she was going to have any fun at all. They couldn't let her waste all her time in museums, all by herself. Jennifer certainly had no intention of joining her in that kind of activity. She couldn't remember ever seeing a photo of a celebrity coming in or out of a museum.

The conveyor belt finally began to move, and moments later their luggage appeared. According to the information Jennifer had received, they'd be met at the airport for transportation to the hotel. She'd imagined a uniformed chauffeur and a stretch limo. But the man holding the *Babes in Manhattan* sign was just a bored-looking man in ordinary clothes, and the mode of transportation was a van. The next disappointment was her first view of the city.

Gazing out at the suburban-style houses and small buildings, she was puzzled.

'This doesn't look like New York.'

'We're not in Manhattan yet,' Megan told her. 'This is Queens, it's a residential area.'

'How do you know?' Erica asked.

'I've been here before,' Megan said. 'When I was eight, with my parents. Which is why I have no intention of visiting the Statue of Liberty or the Empire State Building. Been there, done that.'

'Well, I haven't,' Erica said. 'I'm hoping Danny will show me all the famous sights.'

'I'm going to have a completely different experience this time,' Megan stated. 'Who's going to shop with me?'

Jennifer considered this. 'Can we go to Tiffany's?'

'Are you insane?' Megan shook her head. 'I can't afford jewellery like that, and neither can you.' Her eyes narrowed. 'Why do you want to go there?'

Serena answered for Jennifer. 'Because she might see someone famous.'

Jennifer faked a look of innocence. 'Why do you think that?'

Serena grinned. 'Because I know you. I'll bet you're planning to spend the whole weekend hunting down celebrities.'

'You make me sound like a stalker,' Jennifer said. They were on the freeway now, and there wasn't much to see, so she closed her eyes and leaned back. She must have dozed off, because she was woken up by a collective shriek and cries of 'Look, look!'

Manhattan lay before them, and they all fell silent as they confronted a dazzling blur of lights and colours and people and noise. Jennifer peered out of the window and tried to catch the names of streets. They were on 37th Street, and then they were on Third Avenue. The street numbers climbed higher, and the cab turned onto 50-something, and then turned again onto Madison Avenue. They pulled up in front of the Palladium Hotel, familiar to all of them from the TV show. The hotel wasn't just a place for tourists – its cocktail lounge was a frequent hangout of the 'Babes'.

A uniformed young man opened the door of the van and greeted them in a tone that was less than enthusiastic.

'Welcome to the Palladium.'

He took each girl's hand, one by one, to help them out, and kept repeating 'Welcome to the Palladium' in the same flat voice. Jennifer caught a glimpse of two other uniformed men taking their luggage out and carrying the bags into the hotel. This was luxury, Jennifer thought, not to have to carry your own luggage. She could forget about the economy seats and the lack of a limousine. This was the beginning of her dream-come-true.

But she had no time to revel in the moment. A chic-looking but stony-faced woman hurried towards them and briskly introduced herself as Heather Something from Corona Productions. She didn't give the girls the opportunity to introduce themselves.

'Hurry, girls, we're running late. People are waiting.' She practically shoved them through the hotel's revolving doors.

'It's just like on the show!' Jennifer exclaimed, taking in the ultra-modern black and white lobby.

'Yes, yes, you can look around later,' Heather said. 'The cast is waiting for you.'

'We're meeting them now?' Megan asked in dismay. 'Can't we freshen up first?'

'There's no time,' Heather snapped. 'We're on a tight schedule. Follow me.'

Jennifer frantically and unsuccessfully searched her bag for a compact mirror as they were directed under an archway to the cocktail lounge. Fortunately, the space was dimly lit, but even so she could imagine how bedraggled they all looked compared to the other guests who sat on the stools that lined the shiny black bar. Women in little black dresses or skin-tight blue jeans with stiletto heels. Men in sharp, expensive suits that undoubtedly bore an Italian name on the label. At least Jennifer was in black. The trousers were wrinkled and the T-shirt had been chosen for its loose comfort rather than its style. But it was better than Erica's baggy top with the stain where she'd spilled her drink on the plane. And far better than Serena's terrible leggings and trainers. As they entered, she pulled off the elastic band that was holding her blonde hair back and ran her fingers through it. With no mirror, she could only hope that it looked stylishly tousled and not just messy.

Erica dug her fingers into Jennifer's arm. 'It's *them*,' she squealed. Jennifer groaned. Couldn't her friends fake a modicum of sophistication? But even she was having a hard time keeping her expression under control when she saw the four 'babes', standing at the end of the long bar.

They looked fabulous, of course, just like they did on the show, and even thinner in person. Jennifer took a deep breath, sucked in her stomach and marched over to the actress who played Marina.

'Hello, I'm Jennifer,' she began, but that was as far as she got. Heather grabbed her arm.

'You stand here,' she ordered. Then she thrust a martini glass in Jennifer's hand. She positioned the other girls and gave each of them a glass.

Serena looked worried. 'I think the drinking age in the United States is twenty-one.'

Megan looked exasperated as she raised her glass to her lips.

'Not yet!' Heather shrieked. 'OK, look at the person next to you and smile. George, are you ready?'

'Got it,' a man said. He held a camera up and began shooting. 'Girl in the yellow sweater, stop hunching your shoulders. Katherine, darling, that's fabulous, just tilt your head to the right slightly. Beautiful, Maggie, stay just like that. Blonde, move an inch to the left.'

'My name is Jennifer,' she said, but no one seemed to hear her. The flash of the camera momentarily blinded her, but when her vision cleared, she noticed that none of the other people in the bar were paying any attention to this. She wasn't offended – in fact, it impressed her to see how blasé New Yorkers were. They probably saw celebrities being photographed all the time.

'Now talk and sip your drinks,' Heather ordered them. Jennifer was standing by the woman who played Jane,

Maggie Donner, and Maggie made eye contact.

'Welcome to New York,' she said brightly.

'Thank you,' Jennifer said. 'It's my first trip, and—'

'OK, we've got enough,' the man with the camera bellowed.

'Excellent, thank you all very much,' Heather declared. Suddenly, the four TV stars were being ushered out of the bar. Heather looked back at the new arrivals. 'Have a good time, girls. The receptionist at the desk has some material for you.' And then she was gone too.

'Is that it?' Jennifer asked. 'We didn't even get a chance to talk to them!' She couldn't believe it. She'd visualised so hard!

Megan took a sip of her cocktail and made a face. 'Nasty,' she told them.

That figured, Jennifer thought glumly. Just one more thing that wasn't living up to expectations.

'Can we check in now?' Serena asked wistfully.

They left the lounge and came back into the lobby. Suddenly, for Jennifer, all traces of disappointment evaporated. She froze in place.

'Jen, come on,' Megan urged. 'Jen? Are you OK?'

'Look,' Jennifer whispered. Megan didn't read the same magazines that Jennifer did, but there wasn't a person on the face of the earth who wouldn't recognise

51

the figure that was crossing the lobby.

Even Megan was impressed. 'Is that really Jordan Blake?'

'It most certainly is,' Jennifer murmured. There was no mistaking the tall, lanky singer with the white-blond hair who strode through the lobby, accompanied on each side by a larger and huskier man. Bodyguards, Jennifer assumed. Others in the lobby were doing double-takes as he passed them.

A thrill shot through Jennifer's body. This was a celebrity on a whole different level from the 'Babes'. Quickly, she recalled what she knew about the rock star. He lived in California. That meant he could be staying right here at this hotel.

Erica and Serena were at the reception desk. Jennifer hurried over there.

'Is Jordan Blake at this hotel?' she asked the young man behind the desk.

The man smiled blandly. 'And you are . . ?'

'Jennifer Hawkins, I'm with them,' she said breathlessly. 'Is he staying here? Jordan Blake?'

His smile remained in place. 'I'm sorry, Miss Hawkins, we're not at liberty to divulge information about our guests.'

'So he *is* a guest!'

'I did not say that, Miss Hawkins.'

Jennifer had to accept the fact that she wouldn't be receiving any information from the receptionist. Not now, at least. She looked at his identification badge.

'Nicholas Caine,' she read. 'Do people call you Nick?'

He nodded slightly. 'Yes, my *friends* call me Nick. Would you sign here, Miss Hawkins?'

Jennifer smiled brightly. 'Call me Jennifer,' she said charmingly as she signed.

'I have something for your group,' the receptionist continued, and handed a brown envelope marked 'Corona Productions' to Megan.

Erica broke in. 'Is there a message for me? Erica Douglas?'

The receptionist's expression changed, and now the smile was warmer. 'Yes, Miss Douglas. Not a message, exactly. This.' He reached under the desk and brought out a huge bouquet of flowers.

Erica gasped in joy. 'Oh, it's beautiful!'

Megan was clearly impressed. 'Two dozen long-stemmed red roses! That must have cost a small fortune.'

Erica was searching in the foliage that surrounded the flowers. 'There's no card.'

'Oh, I'm terribly sorry,' Nick-the-receptionist said quickly. 'Here it is.' He handed her a piece of hotel stationary, and then moved away to speak to another one of the reception staff.

Erica read it silently, but the others weren't going to let her get away with that.

'Is it from Danny? What does it say?' Megan demanded.

'He says welcome to New York, and he wants me to meet him tomorrow for lunch.'

Nick came out from behind the desk. 'I can show you to your suite now, ladies.' He took the flowers from Erica and the girls followed him to the lift.

They emerged on the sixth floor, and he led them to a door which he opened with a card key. Then he stepped aside to let them enter first.

'Wow,' Jennifer breathed. They were in a lovely sitting room, spacious and elegantly decorated. At one end there was a dining table and Nick put the flowers down there. He pointed out the two bedrooms – each with two huge beds and its own bathroom – and indicated where their suitcases had been placed. Jennifer's bags were with Serena's in one bedroom, and the suitcases belonging to Megan and Erica were in the other.

Nick showed them how to operate an elaborate control system. They could press buttons to close the curtains, dim the lights, make the rooms warmer or cooler. There were phones in the sitting room, both bedrooms *and* in each bathroom! By now Jennifer had completely recovered from her disappointment with the welcoming cocktails. She was in the lap of luxury, in the very same hotel as Jordan Blake.

As he was leaving, Nick pointed out the room service menu on the table. 'Many of our visitors from overseas enjoy having dinner in their rooms on the first night,' he told them.

'I think that's a brilliant idea,' Megan declared.

'You want to stay in on our first night in New York?' Jennifer asked in dismay.

'I'm exhausted,' Serena said. "I want to unpack my clothes, have a bath and eat something really fattening.' She examined the menu. 'Mmm, barbecue spare ribs, I'll bet that's yummy.'

'Sounds good to me,' Erica said. Serena passed her the menu then went off into the bedroom. Erica glanced at it but then her eyes went to the flowers.

'They're really gorgeous, aren't they? How sweet of him to welcome me like this.'

Jennifer couldn't resist a comment. 'I think it would have been sweeter if he'd shown up in person.'

'*Jennifer!*' Megan chided her.

'It's OK,' Erica said. 'He's a very important person, he can't stop everything just because someone he met on the internet is in town. And we're having lunch tomorrow.'

'Did he say where?' Megan asked but she didn't get an answer. A wailing noise coming from one of the bedrooms sent them all running in.

Serena was standing in front of an open suitcase, her eyes wide. She turned to her friends with an expression of utter despair.

'This isn't my suitcase!'

Chapter Six

When Serena woke up the next morning, it took her a few seconds to realise where she was. There was a sudden moment of sheer exhilaration when she remembered that she was in a suite at the famed Palladium hotel in New York City. But the exhilaration soon evaporated when she recalled opening her suitcase last night.

Why hadn't she noticed that the plain black valise was a little more battered than the new one she'd checked in at the departure airport? Probably because she was wiped out and jet-lagged, or maybe because she'd assumed it had been knocked about during the flight. In any case, it had been a total shock when she lifted the lid and saw – *not* the floral print nightdress she'd placed on top, but something green and shiny and covered with sequins. Green was Serena's least favourite colour. And she had never in her life worn even one tiny sequin.

Erica had tried to calm her down. 'Whoever this belongs to must have picked yours up by mistake too. Check the luggage tag.'

'There isn't one,' Serena told her.

'Then the person who has your suitcase will find your tag.'

But like the owner of this piece of luggage. Serena had neglected to put any sort of identification on her bag. How totally stupid had that been?

'Call the airport,' Megan instructed her. 'I'm sure the other person has called in to report this. Someone there will have a name for you to contact.'

But so far, the airport had not received any reports of anyone else picking up the wrong bag. Serena had to endure a lecture from the baggage claim person about checking the number the airline had affixed to the bag with the number on her ticket – which might prevent something like this from happening in the future but wasn't much help to her now.

She supposed Jennifer was trying to show sympathy when she declared that she would kill herself if anything like that had happened to her. Megan was more helpful, running down to the hotel's gift shop to find her a toothbrush and an extra-large 'I ♥ New York' T-shirt to wear as a nightie. After a good room service dinner and assurances from her friends that she'd get a call from the airport in the morning, she'd soon drifted off to sleep.

Now that she'd slept, she was still anxious, but she was alert and ready to address her situation. At least she had her mates with her, and wasn't alone with her problem.

The other bed in her room was empty and voices were coming from outside the door, so she got out of bed and went into the sitting room. There she found Jennifer and Megan gathered around a table laden with steaming cups, glasses of juice, trays of muffins and other assorted breads.

'Room service breakfast!' Jennifer called out happily.

'Coffee or tea?' Megan offered.

Serena joined them at the table and accepted a coffee. 'Thanks. Now, what are we going to do?'

'I looked through the information from Corona Productions,' Jennifer said. 'There are tickets for a special *Babes in Manhattan* bus tour. We can see all the places where they hang out on the show.'

'Not me,' Megan said. 'Shops open in thirty minutes, and I'm organising my itinerary. I can't decide whether to start uptown and work my way down, or the other way around.'

'I meant, what are we going to do about my suitcase?' Serena asked.

But the girls were more interested in the question Erica asked as she emerged from the bedroom. 'How do I look? Do you think this is right for lunch in a restaurant?'

'Depends on the restaurant,' Megan said. 'Where are you going?'

'I don't know. I'm meeting Danny at his office. Some place called Trump Tower.'

'Ohmigod,' Jennifer exclaimed. 'Donald Trump built that!'

'He couldn't have built it, he's not an architect,' Megan pointed out.

'Well, he commissioned it to be built,' Jennifer said. 'It's a very upscale place.' She turned to Erica. 'Danny's office is in Trump Tower? He must be loaded. How old is he?'

'Our age,' Erica said happily. 'Can you believe it? He's incredibly successful for someone so young.'

'Then you'll be going somewhere classy,' Megan declared. She examined Erica critically. 'That will do. But you need a little scarf or a necklace. Let me see what I've got.'

Serena turned to Erica with pleading eyes. 'If you're not meeting him until lunchtime, can you help me find my suitcase?'

Erica looked torn. 'I *could*, I suppose. I wanted to find a salon this morning and get my hair trimmed. And maybe have a manicure . . .'

Serena sighed. 'That's OK, you go ahead with your plans. There's nothing you can do anyway.' And thank you all very much, she added silently.

'Talk to Nick,' Jennifer suggested.

'Who?'

'The receptionist. I'm sure things like this have happened before to guests. He'll know what to do.'

'And I'll meet you for lunch,' Megan added. 'If your suitcase hasn't turned up by then, we can shop for replacement clothes.' And with that they left her to it.

Serena went back into her room and dressed in the same top and leggings she'd worn the day before. She glared balefully at the suitcase, untouched since she'd opened it. And then it occurred to her that she might find a clue as to its owner among the contents.

She took out the top item. The green sparkly fabric turned out to be an elaborate jewelled gown. Laying it out on the bed and stepping back to examine it, Serena immediately realised something about its owner. She was a big woman – not obese, not even fat necessarily, just large all over. And tall.

It looked like a pretty expensive dress. If it came from a luxury boutique in New York, maybe she could take it there and they'd remember who bought it. She searched the garment for labels but she couldn't find any. Examining the gown closely, she thought that it might be handmade. This person was definitely rich.

Pleased with the way her investigation was going so far, she continued looking through the items in the suitcase. There were more dresses, and all of them elaborate and heavily decorated, grand and formal – this woman obviously went to a lot of fancy events. Serena didn't know much about fashion but she knew expensive clothes when she saw them. There were shoes too – satin ones in the colours to match the gowns. These too were an unusually large size.

Serena ran her hands through the inside pockets of the suitcase, and it was there that she discovered another clue. A torn piece of paper – it looked like a receipt. It had to be an old one, the printing on it had faded, and she couldn't read everything, but she could just make out a name, an imprint from a credit card, perhaps.

Feldman.

So, now she knew that the owner of this suitcase – and the person who most likely had hers – was a heavy-set socialite named Feldman. Too bad she didn't have any friends around with whom she could share this information. They might offer some advice as to what to do next.

But then Jennifer's earlier suggestion came back to her. She grabbed her backpack and the one remaining card key and left the suite.

She was pleased and a little surprised to see a familiar face – Nick-from-the-night-before was still there in the lobby. He nodded at her in recognition.

'Can I help?' he asked as she approached the desk.

'I hope so,' she said, sighing, then noticed he looked a little weary close-up. 'Don't you ever get any time off?'

Despite his tired eyes, he smiled warmly and it transformed his face, all signs of fatigue disappeared.

'Three days on, three days off,' he told her. Lowering his voice, he added, 'Hotel policy. It makes guests more comfortable if they feel like they know the staff.'

She could understand that. Nick's warm manner certainly made *her* feel more comfortable. 'Well, it's a good policy. I'm glad it's you here,' she said. 'I've got a problem, and I need your help.'

'I'll try,' he said. 'You're with the Corona Productions group, aren't you?'

'Yes, we won the *Babes in Manhattan* contest.' She realised how silly that must sound. 'Jennifer entered us, we didn't even know about it till we won.'

'Jennifer,' he repeated. 'That's the blonde one, right?'

Serena nodded. 'The one who was looking for Jordan Blake.'

'I remember,' Nick said. He was still smiling, but it was a different sort of smile now, and Serena recognised it. She'd seen guys smiling like that when Jennifer was around.

'You're going to have a hard time keeping her away from Jordan Blake,' she told him.

There was a twinkle in his eye as he replied, 'I can imagine. Now, how can I help you?'

'It's about my suitcase.' She explained the situation to him. 'I've called the airport and reported it . . .'

'. . . And you won't hear back from them till long after you've returned to England,' Nick finished for her.

'Exactly,' Serena said. 'So I started my own investigation.' She told him what she'd discovered about the owner of the suitcase.

He considered the information. 'Feldman is a pretty common name. But you say the clothes are fancy?'

'Long evening gowns,' Serena said. 'The kind a society woman would wear to a charity ball or something like that.'

Nick turned to his computer and hit some keys. 'I'm searching the phone directory for Feldmans who live on the Upper East Side. That's where a lot of high-society types live.' After a moment, he hit another key and some pages came out of a printer.

'Rather a lot of them, I'm afraid,' Nick said. 'But your calls shouldn't take too long.'

'Thank you,' Serena said, accepting the papers from him. Then she sighed. 'Nice way to spend a holiday in New York. Sitting in a hotel room, calling strangers and asking them if they lost a suitcase.'

Nick winced. He glanced around as if to make sure no one was within hearing distance, and when he finally spoke it was practically a whisper.

'I'm not supposed to tell you this, but using the phone in a hotel room is incredibly expensive. You'd be much better off getting a pay-as-you-go cell phone. There's a place just down the street where you can pick one up for about twenty-five dollars.'

Serena brightened. 'And then I could go to museums and make calls while I walk there!'

'Exactly!' Nick said.

'Thank you, you've been a big help,' she said and put the papers in her bag.

'No problem.' Nick gave her a genuine smile.

Nice guy, she thought. Jennifer was right.

Serena found the mobile phone shop, and picked out a phone that came with one hundred minutes pre-paid. Surely that would be enough, she thought. Walking north, she punched in the first number on the list Nick had given her.

'Hello?'

'May I speak to Mrs Feldman, please?'

'Speaking.'

'Um, I'm looking for a Mrs Feldman who might have lost a suitcase at JFK airport yesterday.'

'I'm afraid you have the wrong Mrs Feldman. I wasn't at the airport yesterday.'

'Thank you, I'm sorry to have bothered you.' Serena pressed the disconnect button and the screen told her she'd used one minute.

Ninety-nine to go, she thought glumly as she entered the next number on the list.

Chapter Seven

Erica emerged from the salon onto Fifth Avenue thirty minutes before she was due to meet Danny. She'd spent almost two hours and a big chunk of her budget for the weekend there, but it had been well worth it. Her red curls were no longer springing off her head like corkscrews – they delicately framed her face, and the beautician had used some kind of product that made her hair gleam. Her nails had been given a perfect French manicure. And when she told the beautician that she was about to meet a young man she'd hooked up with on the internet, she was treated to a free make-up application.

There was no missing Trump Tower – the gleaming structure loomed before her – but she was still too early. She stopped in front of the shop just next to the building, and examined her reflection in the window; she'd never looked so good, so polished. She was still herself, only better.

Which was exactly who she wanted to be. She recalled a novel she'd read a year or two back, some romantic chick-lit, about a man and a woman who had met online in a chat room. They'd both lied like crazy to each other, bragging and inventing and going to the point of posting photos of friends they thought were better-looking than themselves. Neither thought they would ever really meet, or that they might actually like each other – it was all just for laughs. It was a cute story, silly but fun, and of course when they finally met in person and realised what they'd both done, they laughed over it all and fell in love anyway.

But that was a story. This was real life, and Erica was very happy that she'd never considered lying about herself to Danny. Maybe she just didn't have that kind of imagination. Or maybe, somewhere in the back of her mind, she believed that they would actually meet one day and she didn't want to be embarrassed when he learned the truth about her.

But it was even more likely that she just wasn't that kind of person. She might not have the self-confidence that seemed to come so naturally to Megan. She didn't have Jennifer's extraordinary good looks. She wasn't as intelligent as Serena. Her life wasn't what she wanted it to be, but she'd come to accept it. And herself as well. But that didn't make her feel any less nervous about what was about to happen.

She'd been so distracted by her reflection in the window that she hadn't noticed what was behind the glass. She stepped back to admire some of the loveliest jewellery she'd ever seen. Diamond rings, gold necklaces, silver bracelets, all positioned against an eggshell-blue background. Then she realised she was standing in front of Tiffany's.

She'd seen the film, of course – *Breakfast at Tiffany's*, one of the most romantic movies ever, starring her favourite actress in all the world, Audrey Hepburn. She could drum up an image of Audrey, sipping her coffee in the early hours of the morning, standing right where Serena was standing and gazing into the same window. Beautiful, elegant Audrey, who always seemed to say and do the right thing. She was so perfect. Of course, Audrey wasn't on her way to see a guy she'd met online, but she couldn't help wondering – what would Audrey do in her situation? How would she feel, how would she behave? Would she be nervous at the thought of meeting someone whose life, whose world was so much more interesting than her own?

She recalled another Audrey Hepburn movie she'd seen, *Sabrina*. Audrey had played the daughter of a rich family's chauffeur, and she was in love with one of the rich sons. She didn't let the fact that she was the daughter of a servant make her feel unworthy of the rich guy. She handled the whole situation with charm, beauty and confidence. Could Erica ever come up to the standard set by Audrey Hepburn?

But Danny wasn't expecting Audrey Hepburn. Danny had seen her photos. He knew about her less-than-thrilling life, her lack of life experience, the kind of menial work she did. And he still wanted to meet her in person. Still, it wouldn't hurt to keep Audrey in mind, and try to emulate the poise, the elegant quality, the feminine demeanour. And if she was intimidated by Danny's success, by his business suit or his super-confident and self-assured manner, she'd somehow manage to keep it to herself.

She checked her watch. It was just about time. Taking a deep breath, she made her way towards the Tower. For a moment, she felt lost in the waves of people moving in and out of the massive building. Men, women, children . . . she kept her eyes on the main door and narrowly avoided crashing into a man with a briefcase, a tourist with a camera. She tried to prepare herself mentally. There had to be some kind of directory in the lobby that would tell her which floor he was on. She'd find the lift. Then she would have to speak to some secretary, and she'd be asked what kind of business she had with Mr Parsons. What would she say: lunch?

She was so lost in her thoughts and intent on getting to the entrance without any accident that she didn't see him, and would have passed right by him if he hadn't spoken.

'Erica?'

She froze, and then she turned her head. 'Danny?'

He smiled. 'Hi.'

She smiled back. 'Hello.'

She didn't know he'd be so tall. Other than that, he was just like his photo. Tousled brown hair, square jaw, a nose that some might consider slightly long but which fit his face. Casually dressed in combat trousers, a striped shirt, a denim jacket. No one would guess that he was a tycoon, a wheeler-dealer, whatever they called people who did the kind of work he did. She liked this.

'I recognised you right away,' he said. 'You look like your picture.'

'So do you,' she said. 'I guess I just expected you to look more . . . more business-like.'

'Like in a suit?' He grinned. 'It's casual Friday. Kind of a tradition in the business world – the one day in the week you can dress casually for the office.'

There was a moment of silence. And then the weirdness of it all caught up with her. A giggle rose up in her throat. She tried to force it back down but it was no use. She burst out laughing, which was something she was sure Audrey Hepburn would never do.

But Danny didn't seem to mind. After a split second of surprise, his smile widened and then he was laughing too.

'I know, this is crazy,' he said. 'I mean, like, what do we do now? Shake hands? No, wait, you're European. We're supposed to kiss each other on both cheeks, right?'

'That's the French, not the English,' Erica informed him. Then, with a boldness she didn't know she possessed, she asked, 'How about a hug?'

'Sounds good to me.'

They embraced, quickly and not too tightly. His arms felt strong and gentle at the same time, and after the hug, it seemed only natural that he would take her hand.

'We're going to lunch at a restaurant on the upper west side,' he told her. 'OK if we walk?'

'Sure.' She had no idea where or how far away the

upper west side was, but it didn't matter to her. She was just so relieved to find the person she'd expected and hoped to find. He might be a high-powered businessman, but he certainly didn't fit the stereotype.

She glanced back at the building. There must have been over fifty storeys in the shiny, modern tower. 'You have an amazing office,' she said.

He shrugged a little awkwardly. 'It's a central location,' he said. 'So it's convenient.'

'But it's a pretty famous building, isn't it?'

He nodded. 'There's this reality TV show here where people try to get Donald Trump to hire them. It's filmed in this building.'

'We've got that show in the UK too,' Erica told him. 'What floor are you on?'

He hesitated, as if he couldn't remember right away. 'Twenty-third,' he said finally.

'So you must have a nice view.'

Danny shrugged again. 'It's OK.' He grinned. 'There's only one window and it's pretty small, so I don't look out much.'

She seriously doubted that any windows in a building like this would be small, but she liked that he wasn't trying to impress her. They crossed the street in silence.

'How do you like New York so far?' he asked once

they were on the other side of Fifth Avenue.

'I like it,' she said. 'It's big.' And then she wanted to kick herself. How stupid was that? 'Actually, I haven't seen that much of it yet.' There was more silence. This was getting uncomfortable.

She looked at the building they were passing. Uniformed doormen were opening the doors of taxis in front of a grand-entrance.

'That looks like an important place,' she said.

'The Plaza Hotel,' Danny told her. 'That's where the Beatles stayed when they came to the US for the first time in the 60s. They were English too.' He blushed slightly. 'Boy, that was a dumb thing to say. Like you wouldn't know the Beatles were English.'

She looked up at him with a smile. He was feeling just as awkward as she was! It only made him more appealing. Now, what could she say about the Beatles?

'They were from Liverpool.' Then it was her turn to go pink. *Everyone* knew the Beatles came from Liverpool. Now they'd both said dumb things. That was kind of nice, in a weird way.

Danny nodded. 'Have you ever been to Liverpool?'
'No.'

Another silence. Frantically, Erica tried to think of a new topic. Happily, something came right to mind.

'The roses were beautiful,' she said.

'What roses?'

'The ones you sent to me, at the hotel!'

For a second he looked confused, but then his face cleared. 'Oh, right! The flowers. Were you, um, pleased with them?'

'Of course I was,' she replied. 'Did I mention on Friendspace that roses are my favourite flowers?'

'I guess so . . .' he said and coloured a little. 'Anyway, I'm glad you like them . . .'

'Very much,' she said. 'Thank you.'

'You're welcome,' he replied.

Silence again. This is ridiculous, Erica thought. We've 'talked' like crazy online, about everything. Why can't we think of anything to say now?

Danny read her mind. 'This is weird,' he said suddenly. 'We had no problem telling each other stuff on the Internet, so why aren't we talking now?'

'I know!' Erica exclaimed, relieved. Impulsively, she squeezed his hand. He squeezed back.

And then it all got easier. They passed Central Park and admired the horse-drawn carriages.

'I love horses,' she told him.

'Me too,' he said. 'Do you ride?'

'I've never been on a horse in my life,' she admitted.

He grinned. 'Me neither.'

Something in common! This merited another hand squeeze.

They walked along a path through the park, passing joggers, playing children, people picnicking on the grass.

'You're lucky to work so close to this,' Erica told him. 'So beautiful. And free!' Again, she wanted to kick herself. It wasn't like he had to worry about paying for stuff.

But Danny nodded with enthusiasm. 'Very true. Sometimes, on nice days like this, I buy a hot dog and a soda from one of those stands and eat my lunch right here.'

'We could do that now,' Erica suggested.

'No, I want to take you some place special for your first lunch in New York,' he said.

Special was an understatement. She'd worried that they might be going to one of those stuffy, pretentious places where she wouldn't know which fork to use for each course. But immediately on entering the restaurant, which was called Zest, Erica could see that this was a totally modern place; informal and very trendy. Just as expensive as the fussy, fancy places, but young, hip and fun. A real *Babes in Manhattan* kind of restaurant.

And the people occupying the tables suited the surroundings. Everyone looked stylish and cool, casual but elegantly pulled together. Even the maître d' was good-looking. He approached them with a warm smile.

'Good afternoon, Mr Parsons. Your table is ready.'

So Danny didn't eat all his meals in Central Park. Clearly, he was a regular at this upscale eatery. Erica followed the man to a table for two, and slipped into the chair he pulled out for her.

'Is this all right for you?' Danny asked. 'I mean, you're in the business, you know all about restaurants.' He actually sounded anxious, like he was afraid it might not be up to Erica's standards. She hastened to set him straight.

'I know about *one* restaurant,' she told him. 'And you can't compare it to this place.'

'Really? It's not any good?'

'Oh, it's perfectly nice,' she assured him. 'Just a very ordinary Italian restaurant. Spaghetti bolognese, veal parmigiana, the usual stuff.' She accepted a menu from a waiter. 'Nothing like this.'

'This is an Italian restaurant,' Danny pointed out.

'Not like La Trattoria,' Erica said. She perused the menu. 'Scampi Fra Diavolo. Pumpkin Ravioli. Steamed sea bass.' She grinned. 'My uncle wouldn't know a sea bass if it swam into his mouth.'

'Can't you put new things on the menu?' Danny asked. 'Maybe this place will give you some ideas. And if your uncle is the owner, you must have some influence.'

Her smile faded. She really didn't want to talk about her job, it was just too depressing.

'Tell me about *your* work,' she urged. 'It must be exciting.'

He shrugged. 'Buying, selling, trading . . . it's boring. I'd rather talk about food.' He paused. 'Or you.' He cocked his head to one side and gazed at her thoughtfully. 'You know, when I said you look just like your picture, I wasn't really telling the truth. You look even prettier.'

'So do you,' she blurted out. 'I mean, even nicer.' She could feel her face burning. Quickly, she turned and pretended to be looking around at the other diners. Then she drew in her breath.

'Ohmigod, is that Taylor Lautner?'

'Who?'

'The actor from those *Twilight* movies!'

'I've never seen them,' he admitted. 'But it could well be him. We get a lot of celebrities here.'

Danny must really come to this restaurant all the time, she thought. He spoke as if he belonged here. She looked again at the young man sitting at the corner table.

'If you walk towards the restrooms, you could get a better look at him,' Danny told her.

'No, it's fine,' she said quickly. What would he think if she added, 'I'd rather look at you'? Out loud, she said, 'I'm not *that* interested . . . But if Jennifer was here, she'd absolutely die!'

'Who's Jennifer?'

'One of my friends. She was the one who entered the competition. She's crazy about celebrities.'

'Yeah? Tell me about the competition.'

Erica explained about *Babes in Manhattan*, and how she and her friends watched the show every week. That led her to tell him about the individual girls and what made each of them unique. And he didn't seem to find any of it silly or stupid. He nodded and laughed and urged her on. They ordered their meals, the food came, they ate, and they never stopped talking.

It was just what she'd hoped for; exactly what she'd fantasised. They were connected. Like being on Friendspace. Only better.

Chapter Eight

'And on your right,' the guide intoned in a flat voice, 'you will see the boutique that was featured in season one, episode twelve.'

A woman on the bus spoke up excitedly. 'Was that the one where Kelsey bought the dress that was too small, because it was on sale? And she went on a crash diet so she could get into it for a party?'

The guide looked at her blankly, but another passenger provided the answer. 'No, it's the one when Marina loses her credit card.'

Jennifer remembered the episode, and she could have corrected the second passenger. Marina didn't actually lose her credit card. She'd given the salesgirl a card but the card had been maxed out so it was rejected, and the salesgirl had taken it away from her. But she didn't say anything. By this point, she'd realised she had nothing in common with the other people taking the *Babes in Manhattan* tour. They just wanted to gape and gawk. They didn't seem to have any ambitions other than that.

Jennifer, on the other hand, was taking notes, jotting down the addresses. She'd hoped they would be able to get off the bus and explore the places on their own, but the bus wasn't stopping at any of the sites. In many ways, this tour was shaping up to be a major disappointment. She'd seen the outside of shops, restaurants, bars, clubs and the luxurious apartment building where the character Tori supposedly lived. But she hadn't seen even one celebrity.

She had to remind herself that the TV show didn't necessarily represent real life. Maybe the really important people didn't even hang out at these places. She only had three days in New York, and this bus tour had already taken up two hours of it. As far as she was concerned, this was turning out to be a total waste of time.

She rose from her seat and went to the front of the bus. 'I want to get off now,' she told the tour guide.

'You can't,' he said. 'We're not making any stops.'

A red light appeared in front of the bus. 'You're stopping now,' she informed him.

'You can't get off in the middle of the tour,' he

81

informed her. 'It's against the rules.'

She thought quickly, and raised her voice. 'But . . . I'm sick! In fact, I think I'm about to throw up!'

The driver turned and looked at the tour guide in alarm. The guide just stared at her, but the driver took action. He pulled on a lever and the bus doors automatically opened.

She hopped off, dodged a taxi and made it to the pavement – or the sidewalk as they called it over here. Now what? Roam the streets and keep her eyes open? She had absolutely no idea where she was.

She dug into her bag, searching for the map that Nick-the-receptionist had given her. He was a sweetie, that Nick, and pretty hot, too. If she wasn't on the hunt for bigger prey, she wouldn't mind flirting a bit with *him*.

Finally, she located the map. Now, where was she? She'd thought the bus tour would provide clues as to celebrity hang-outs, but that hadn't panned out. She had no idea where to begin her search.

She looked for a sign that would identify the street where she was standing, and saw that it had two names: Sixth Avenue and Avenue of the Americas. She looked for it on the map, and realised this particular avenue ran practically the whole length of Manhattan. She walked a bit to get the name of the cross street, but before she reached it, a restaurant on the other side of the street caught her eye. On the green awning, the name was spelled out in lower case letters: bar pitti.

Now, why did she know that name? She reached back into her bag and pulled out the magazine she'd been reading on the plane yesterday. Yes, there it was! A photo of one of her favourite singers, with the caption: 'Beyonce enjoying lunch with friends on the terrace of Bar Pitti.'

She dashed to the corner and crossed the street. The pavement terrace of the restaurant was packed, and there was no hope of her getting a seat there. Besides, it was probably way too expensive for her. But it didn't matter. She could just hang out on the pavement and search the faces of the diners.

There was no sign of Beyoncé. But that streaky-long-haired guy with the huge dimples – wasn't that the actor who played Sawyer in *Lost*? And that tiny dark-haired woman at another table – Jen was almost positive it was Gabrielle from *Desperate Housewives*'. If only she'd take off her sunglasses . . .

Jennifer edged closer to get a better look at the streaky-haired man. But suddenly, another man stood in her way.

'Excuse me, Miss, are you interested in a table?'

She barely glanced at him. 'No, thanks, I'm just looking.'

'Well, I'm afraid I'm going to have to ask you to move on.'

Now she looked at him. His grey uniform-type suit told her he was a waiter. She offered him one of her special smiles. 'I'm not bothering anyone, am I?'

He didn't return her smile. 'Not yet,' he said stonily. 'But our patrons don't like to be stared at.'

'I'm not staring, I'm just looking,' Jennifer protested. But the waiter obviously didn't understand the difference. He shook his head.

Clearly, he wasn't going to be any help in identifying celebrities. And he definitely wasn't going to let her get any closer to them. She walked to the corner and looked up at the street sign. Bleecker Street . . . that was familiar, too. Out came the magazine again.

Yes, there was the photo – Blake Lively from *Gossip Girl* coming out of some place called Magnolia Bakery on Bleecker Street. She could even see the street number on the awning above the bakery – 401. She turned to the left and started walking.

The building itself was nothing much, just battered-looking red brick. What made it remarkable was the queue waiting to get in. It stretched from the door of the bakery to around the corner. Slowly, she moved alongside the line of people and checked out every face. Nobody looked famous to her. But it dawned on her that celebrities wouldn't have to wait in line like ordinary people. Someone like Blake Lively would be ushered inside as soon as she arrived.

She hurried back to the door.

'Hey, get in line!' someone yelled.

'I'm just looking,' Jennifer called back. Honestly, was looking a crime in New York City? The door opened and practically hit her in the face as a woman came out of the bakery. She didn't look like anyone important, and Jennifer only had seconds to check out the people who were inside. She *did* get a whiff of a deliciously sugary scent which almost made her want to join the queue.

But she knew she'd have to wait ages to get inside, and really, what was the point? Blake Lively couldn't come to a bakery very often with a body like that. Jennifer didn't want to spend an hour and just end up with a cupcake, no matter how yummy it might be. She didn't have all that long in New York, and she had more important things to do.

And then something hit her. She *did* know where one celebrity might be. She turned and started back uptown.

Forty-five minutes later she was back in the Palladium.

She did a quick scan of the lobby, but the object of her quest wasn't there. Checking her watch, she saw that it was twelve-thirty. Lunchtime. Maybe he was in the hotel restaurant.

There were plenty of people in the booths and at the tables of the restaurant. She marched all around the room and ignored the man who kept asking, 'May I help you, Miss? Table for one?' She spotted no one of any interest. She checked the bar too, but that was practically empty. She supposed it was a bit early for cocktails, even for celebrities. Back in the lobby, she saw Nick behind the desk. Maybe he knew where famous people ate lunch.

'Hello,' she greeted him. 'Remember me? I'm Jennifer, I checked in yesterday.'

He smiled. 'Of course I remember you.'

Jennifer recalled the fuss she'd made about wanting to know if Jordan Blake was in the hotel.

Or maybe Nick remembered her for another reason. He was certainly looking very friendly for someone she must have annoyed the evening before. She did her trademark hair toss, a move she'd perfected years ago. It required a quick shake of the head so her blonde waves would bounce around her shoulders, punctuated by wide eyes and an even wider smile. This usually worked pretty well when she wanted something from a guy.

And it definitely seemed to be working now. She could swear she saw the light of interest in Nick's eyes. They were very attractive eyes too, she noted. A light, clear blue colour, framed by long black lashes . . .

But she didn't have time to waste admiring a receptionist's eyes. 'I was just wondering if you could recommend some restaurants.'

'Of course,' he said. 'What kind of food do you like? Our own restaurant serves highly regarded new American cuisine. There's an excellent Chinese restaurant just around the corner, and if you like French food . . .'

She shook her head briskly. 'No, I'm looking for restaurants with a certain kind of clientele.'

For a moment he looked puzzled, and then his expression cleared. 'Ah, yes, I remember. You want to see celebrities.'

'Exactly!' Jennifer said. So Nick was sharp, too! He was clearly wasted as a hotel receptionist.

Nick took out a map and began marking it with a pencil. 'Over here on East 65th is Daniel. This is considered to be one of the best restaurants in New York, it's got three stars, and you could very well see famous faces having lunch. Or if you walk over to Central Park

West, there's Jean George. That's a very popular place.'

'Have *you* ever been there?' Jennifer asked him.

He laughed. 'No, I'm afraid my salary wouldn't permit that.' He looked at her thoughtfully. 'These are very expensive restaurants.'

'Oh, I'm not planning to eat there,' she assured him. 'I just want to hang out around there.'

'Well, that might be a little difficult,' Nick told her. 'Restaurants don't take kindly to people just hanging out without eating or drinking.'

'Not even if I waited outside and watched people go in and out?'

Nick shook his head. 'Restaurants like Daniel have doormen. They'll make you move on.'

Just like at Bar Pitti. Jennifer frowned. This was going to be harder than she thought it would be.

'What about shopping,' she began, but Nick was now distracted by a couple staggering towards the desk. The man's tie had come undone and his eyes were half-closed. The woman tottered on her stiletto heels and her big hair was all over the place. But even in her messy state, Jennifer could identify the fabulous dress she wore as something that could have come straight off the catwalk. She examined the two of them to ascertain if either might be a somebody, but she didn't recognise them. They'd obviously been out all night and were just returning.

'May I help you?' Nick asked cheerfully.

'How late does your room service serve breakfast?' the man said, a little blearily.

Nick discreetly ignored their bedraggled condition and spoke smoothly. 'We have a twenty-four-hour room service, sir. You may order any meal you want at any time of the day.'

The words 'room service' set off sparks in Jennifer's mind. But of course! Being a rock star, Jordan Blake had probably been out partying all night too. Right this very minute, he could be waking up and ordering a room service breakfast.

Before Nick could return his attention to her, she took off. Hurrying through the lobby, she turned down each corridor that led off it and looked for signs. Behind a door marked 'Employees only' she found stairs. And after walking down a few steps, she heard a noise that very much sounded like the rattling of dishes, and some very pleasant odours began to reach her nose. It dawned on her that she was hungry. As she approached what she assumed was the hotel kitchen, she noticed a table with some trays covered by white cloths.

A woman came out of the kitchen, went to the table

and checked a little tag sitting on one of the trays. Then she saw Jennifer, and frowned.

'Oh, I must have taken the wrong stairs,' Jennifer chirped, and hurried back to the staircase. Halfway up, she paused and looked over the railing. The woman had picked up a tray, and now she was entering a service lift just across from the kitchen door. Jennifer waited until the lift doors closed, and then ran back to the table where the other trays were waiting.

Quickly, she checked the tags. Each one carried a name and a number, which Jennifer presumed was a room number. And there it was: Blake. But instead of a number, there were two letters: PH.

She snatched the tray and went to the lift, all the while looking over her shoulder and praying no one else would come out of the kitchen. The lift doors opened, and she went in. Examining the buttons on the lift wall, she saw that they all carried numbers except for one that was labelled 'penthouse'. Penthouse. PH. She pressed that one.

She couldn't resist taking a peek under the white cloth. There was a basket of toasted bread and some butter in the shape of a rose, a bowl of cut-up fruits, silverware wrapped in a white cloth napkin. And a plate with a metal lid covering it. She lifted the lid and her mouth watered at the sight of a beautifully rolled omelette and crisp bacon. She couldn't help herself – she took one rasher of bacon and popped it into her mouth.

The lift stopped, and she managed to get the lid back onto the plate before the doors opened. The hallway on the penthouse floor looked quite a bit different from the floor where they were staying. Instead of a plain grey carpet, this floor was covered with something patterned and oriental looking. The lights on the walls were encased in golden cages. There were paintings on the walls too. Jennifer bet that Serena could identify them as real art. And instead of a series of doors, there was only one grand-looking double door.

Taking a deep breath, she marched over to it and knocked. Desperately, she wished she'd taken time in the lift to check herself out in her mirror. She was about to come face-to-face with a major rock star, and she had no idea how she would appear to him. But then she recalled the expression on Nick's face when she'd approached the desk, and she knew she couldn't look too bad.

She heard footsteps coming from the other side of the door, and she held her breath. Then the door opened, and her breath came out in a rush. She was not facing

Jordan Blake. The man in the doorway was short, pudgy and balding.

'Oh, I must have the wrong room,' Jennifer blurted out.

'Who are you looking for?' the man barked impatiently.

'Jordan Blake. I have his room service breakfast.'

'I'll take it,' the man said, extending his hands.

But Jennifer took a step backwards. 'And you are?'

'George Allsop, I'm Mr Blake's agent.' He reached for the tray, but Jennifer took another step back.

'Um, I'm afraid I can't give it to you. Hotel policy, you see. I have to deliver the tray personally to the person who ordered it.'

'*I* ordered the breakfast for Mr Blake,' the agent declared.

'Well, OK, maybe, but Mr Blake's name is on the tag. So I have to give it to him.'

The man's eyes narrowed suspiciously. 'Who are you?'

It dawned on Jennifer that the woman with the tray she'd seen outside the kitchen had been wearing a white uniform. And she certainly hadn't had a leather bag dangling from her shoulder. She smiled nervously.

From behind the man at the door came another voice. 'Yo, George. That my breakfast?'

She recognised the voice immediately and brushed

past the agent so quickly he couldn't stop her. 'Yes, Mr Blake, it's your breakfast!' she sang out.

She only got a glimpse of the famous star as he crossed the sitting room. 'Put it on my bed,' he called over his shoulder before disappearing into another room. Jennifer carried the tray into a bedroom where the floor was littered with clothes, shopping bags and a couple of empty champagne bottles. She laid the tray on the unmade bed, and then went into the adjoining bathroom to check her reflection. Satisfied with that, she checked out the products on the shelves. A cologne that smelled like sandalwood, an expensive body lotion and shampoo set. She touched a crumpled bath towel on the floor and imagined it wrapped around Jordan's wet, naked body. Then, hearing voices, she went back into the bedroom and waited for Jordan to return.

But it wasn't Jordan who came into the bedroom seconds later. Nick entered, and looked at Jennifer sadly. 'Miss Hawkins. I've had a complaint about you,' he said sternly.

She automatically did a head toss, but it didn't seem to have any effect on Nick this time.

'What are you doing here?' he asked.

'Well, I happened to see this tray, with his name on it, and, and I thought it would be OK if I dropped it off here . . .' her voice trailed off as she realised how lame she sounded.

'Come on,' Nick said firmly, though the hand that took her arm was gentle.

Jennifer had no choice. She bowed her head as she left the room, so she couldn't get much of a look at the sitting room. Jordan was nowhere to be seen. But George Allsop was still there, and he glared harshly at Jennifer before turning his attention to Nick.

'Thank you for coming so quickly,' he said, and pressed something into the receptionist's hand. A tip, Jennifer presumed. She walked out of the penthouse suite with Nick close behind.

'That was a bad idea,' he said, shaking his head as they waited for the lift.

'I know . . . but I just wanted to meet him,' Jennifer said miserably.

She thought she caught a glimmer of a smile on his face. 'Well, I have to admit, that was a pretty gutsy way of going about it.'

She bit her lip. 'Are you going to have me thrown out of the hotel?'

'I should,' Nick said. 'But I won't. As long as you promise not to do anything like that again.'

'I promise,' Jennifer said. A wave of depression fell

over her. She'd now blown her one big chance to form a relationship with a real celebrity. The lift doors opened and they stepped in together.

'I'm really sorry,' she said and forced a smile. 'I hope he gave you a big tip.'

Nick reached in his pocket and took out what the agent had given him. 'Tickets to Jordan Blake's concert tonight at Madison Square Garden. VIP seats.'

'Golly,' Jennifer breathed. 'Lucky you.'

'Would you like to come with me?' Nick asked without hesitating.

She was so stunned, they'd reached the main floor before she was able to form the word 'Yes.'

Chapter Nine

Had she died and gone to heaven?

Megan recalled a conversation she'd once had with her friends. None of them were particularly religious, but for some reason they'd started talking about how they imagined heaven and hell. She couldn't remember everything they'd come up with, but she knew what she had called heaven: finding herself surrounded by fabulous shops, with the time and the money to enjoy each one. She only had a couple of shopping days in New York, and her purchases couldn't exceed the limit on her credit card, but roaming the streets of Soho in downtown Manhattan was as close to heaven as she'd ever been.

Megan liked to think her own personal style was eclectic – sometimes she wanted to look cool and classic, other times she indulged her more daring side. The lovely boutiques catered to every possible style. At Betsey Johnson on Wooster Street, she found an adorably feminine poufy frock which would stand out at a party. On Prince Street, she discovered J. Crew, where she bought a pair of khaki trousers that would work perfectly on visits to the countryside. Kate Spade on Broome Street was to-die-for – the cutest little handbags she'd ever seen, as much fun as Lulu Guinness but classier.

And there weren't just clothes to admire. Broadway offered Crate and Barrel, items for the home which were the epitome of simple chic. And there was Dean and Deluca, a food store with the most gorgeous edibles. But it was back to clothes when she emerged with her slice of cheesecake and spotted Prada across the street.

Then it was a short walk over to the East Village. East 9th Street was lined with vintage clothing stores, but they were nothing like the second-hand stores she knew at home. These boutiques held no charity shop tat. She saw dresses, scarves, shoes, all from some of the most famous couture houses. And she couldn't resist a 60s miniskirt printed with huge abstract flowers in fluorescent pink and orange. It looked just like vintage Pucci.

One of Megan's first purchases had been a large plain, canvas tote bag which she'd planned to use for carrying all her other purchases, but she'd long since exceeded the bag's capacity. She was now juggling way too many bags. Fortunately, she'd arranged to meet Serena for lunch at the hotel, so she could drop these bags in their room before hitting the uptown stores.

Serena was waiting for her in a booth at the restaurant. There was a dreamy smile on her face and she seemed to be positively glowing, so Megan assumed she'd been successful in her search for the suitcase. But then she realised Serena was still wearing the same scruffy clothes she'd worn on the plane.

'What happened?' Megan asked as she slid into her seat. 'Didn't you find it?'

'Of course I found it,' Serena said. 'It's right on Fifth Avenue.'

'Your suitcase was on Fifth Avenue?'

Serena rolled her eyes. 'No, silly. The Metropolitan Museum of Art. Oh, Megan, it's utterly amazing. I stood right in front of paintings by artists I've only seen on slides. Cézanne, Monet . . . Megan, I saw "Aristotle with a Bust of Homer"!'

'Who?'

'Rembrandt, 1653. I wrote a paper about that painting, Megan! And now I've actually really truly seen it! There's so much at that museum, it's huge, I have to go back. I didn't even get to the American collection.' She sighed. 'New York is truly paradise.'

'I was thinking the same thing,' Megan said, 'for different reasons. But what about your suitcase?'

Serena's blissful smile faded. 'No luck.' Megan listened to her description of what she'd discovered from searching the suitcase that morning. It appeared from the clues Serena found that the owner was a woman named Feldman who wore very expensive and fancy gowns.

'I must have talked to twenty women named Feldman. None of them has lost a suitcase. But I'm waiting for callbacks from some, and I've still got at least fifty more to call.'

Megan considered the situation. 'What kind of evening dresses?' she asked. 'Trendy or frumpy?'

'I'm not sure. What difference would it make?'

'It would narrow the field, if you know the kind of woman you're looking for. If she's a real society person, you could google her. You might find some photos and a first name.'

'Maybe you could take a look at the clothes,' Serena suggested. 'You know more about fashion than I do.'

'Don't you want to make some purchases to tide

you over till you find your own things?' Megan asked hopefully.

'I could definitely use some underwear,' Serena admitted.

Megan eyed the rumpled sweatshirt in distaste. 'You need more than that.'

When they finished lunch, they went back to their suite, where Megan dumped her bags and then joined Serena to examine the suitcase contents. Megan confirmed what Serena had decided.

'Yes, they're expensive and they're handmade,' Megan told her. But she had something else to add.

'And they're in very bad taste.'

'Really?' Serena asked in surprise.

'They're so gaudy,' Megan pointed out. 'Nobody with any sense or style wears glittery tat like this.'

'What about Lady Gaga?' Serena suggested.

'Not in these sizes,' Megan pointed out.

'OK,' Serena sighed. 'Let's go find a computer and we can start searching.'

Aghast, Megan shook her head. There was no way she'd waste valuable shopping time on the internet. 'First, we need to get you something to wear,' she declared firmly. 'You can't wander around New York in a sweatshirt. You shouldn't even hang out in this hotel wearing clothes like that.'

Serena nodded reluctantly. 'I just bought a ticket for the opera tonight. What I'm wearing really wouldn't be appropriate.'

'Then we definitely need to go shopping,' Megan declared.

This was better than searching the internet, but personally, she felt like she was making a great sacrifice for her friend. Megan knew Serena didn't have the kind of budget she had. She wouldn't have the same limit on her credit card – if she even had a credit card. So that meant putting off the uptown shops on Madison and Fifth Avenues. She checked her 'Shopping Guide to New York City' and decided they should hit Macy's on 42nd Street, a huge department store that was described as having reasonable prices.

She thought it might be amusing to fit Serena out in some nice clothes, but it turned out to be more frustrating than fun. Serena totally rejected all Megan's suggestions, refusing to even try on the items Megan chose for her.

'That's not my style,' she kept saying.

'Serena, you don't *have* a style!' Megan pointed out.

Serena wasn't insulted. She just smiled benignly, and selected a simple, inexpensive brown skirt, two jersey tops in beige and khaki, a brown jumper and the plainest underwear available. 'It's not like anyone's going to see it,' she said.

Megan looked a little exasperated.

Next they went to the footwear department, and Megan pointed out some fabulous stilettos. 'Those would give you some height.'

'I'm not going to limp through Manhattan for the sake of three additional inches,' Serena told her.

'How about boots?' Megan suggested. 'Look at those tan suede ones, they'd work nicely with the skirt.'

'And if it rains, they'll be ruined,' Serena replied.

Megan groaned. 'Serena, must you be so practical all the time?'

As usual, Serena ignored the criticism and all Megan's suggestions. Ultimately, she chose plain, flat ballerinas.

And that was it. She wasn't interested in any accessories, not even a bag. She was too anxious to get back to the museum

At least outfitting Serena hadn't taken too long, and now she was free to go to the uptown, upscale stores. And she did, with a vengeance. As if trying to make up for lost time or set a personal best record, she hit the shops running.

First she went into Bloomingdale's on Third Avenue.

It was another big department store, like Macy's, but with a trendier feel. She bought several items in the huge make-up area – she didn't really need them, but now she could walk around with one of Bloomingdale's famous little brown bags.

She walked west on 58th Street so she could stop at Bergdorf Goodman. According to her guide, this store had an enormous shoe department, and she had no problem finding a pair – mauve stilettos with a crystal buckle.

Then it was over to Barneys on Madison Avenue – and, oh, how jealous would Jennifer be! Just as the doorman opened the door for her, she spotted Lindsay Lohan coming out through the revolving door next to her. And once inside, walking through the jewellery department, she was pretty sure that the very skinny blonde with huge sunglasses who was peering into a glass cabinet was one of the Olsen twins.

But again, it was the clothes she was most interested in, and she headed to the famous floor where there had to be every brand of jeans ever made. She bought three pairs: skinny, cropped and boyfriend-style, which she didn't really care for but they were right on trend this season. She didn't mind being a fashion victim.

On another floor she found the perfect LBD – little

black dress – which cost more than all the LBDs already in her wardrobe at home put together. And that required another pair of shoes – strappy-bronze sandals.

From Barneys, she went to a store that often got a mention on *Gossip Girl* – Henri Bendel, on Fifth Avenue. That was where she saw a handbag that literally made her step back and gasp. To call the burned orange alligator satchel an 'it' bag was the understatement of the century. She'd only seen the bag once before, in the *Vogue* magazine she'd perused on the flight to New York, where it had been hailed as the most important fashion accessory since the Hermès scarf or the classic Chanel flap bag. It was beyond beautiful.

Tentatively, she looked at the price tag, and that made her gasp too. She couldn't do the actual maths in her head, but she knew the purchase of this bag would bring her precariously close to her credit limit, and just might exceed it. For a moment, she had the uneasy vision of the salesperson taking her card away, just as it happened to Marina on *Babes in Manhattan*. But surely all the charges she'd made today hadn't yet been tabulated by the bank in the UK that had issued the card. The worst that could happen would be a nasty letter when she got back home.

The bag was ridiculously expensive, and she certainly

didn't need it, she'd only just bought herself a new bag, after all. But how could she pass up this opportunity? When would she have the chance to buy it again? She would never see it in her hometown – it probably wasn't even on sale in London yet. And the joy of feeling that magnificent object dangling from her arm was priceless. She had to have it.

A saleswoman magically appeared at her side. 'It's a beauty, isn't it?'

She was only trying to make a sale, of course, but Megan felt like she now had a sympathetic ally. 'Yes, it's absolutely gorgeous.'

The woman must have heard her accent and realised she wasn't a local. 'You know, if you're going to be taking this out of the country within a month, you'll get a tax refund at the airport.'

That settled the matter. 'I'll take it,' she told the saleswoman.

The woman lifted the bag gently, as if it were a piece of priceless art, and Megan approved of the way she treated with the respect it deserved. She followed her to a counter, where the woman placed the bag in a velvet sack. She then proceeded to wrap it all in massive amounts of tissue paper.

'And how will you be paying for this?'

'By credit card,' Megan said. She reached into the ordinary 'it' bag that currently hung from her shoulder. She fumbled around, and then she frowned. Placing her bag on the counter, she rummaged through it. Then, for the third time in less than fifteen minutes, she gasped.

The saleswoman stopped wrapping. 'Is there a problem?'

'My wallet!' Megan cried out. 'It's gone!' She spoke so loudly that several other customers turned to look at her. Then they all edged away, as if she had a contagious disease.

'Are you sure?' the woman asked.

Megan took out her diary, her make-up case, her keys. She removed item after item until the handbag was completely empty.

'Your pockets?' the woman suggested.

But her leather jacket only produced a crumpled tissue and some coins. A cold, hard shiver shot through Megan. 'I – I've been robbed!'

The saleswoman seemed to be attempting a look of sympathy but she wasn't very successful. 'Yes, pickpockets are a serious problem in New York,' she murmured as she rapidly began the unwrapping process.

'But what should I do?' Megan wailed.

'You should alert your credit card companies and

notify your bank,' the woman said crisply. She lifted the bag and carried it back to the place where Megan found it. Then she moved away to speak to another customer.

Frantically, Megan shoved the contents back into her bag, grabbed her other purchases and ran out of the store. Her panic was rising as she searched the street for someone to help her. When she spotted a young male police officer, she ran towards him yelling, 'Officer, officer! Help me, please!'

There were screams from other people on the street, and several ducked or ran into shops. The policeman whirled round and whipped a gun out of his holster. With his other hand, he pushed Megan under the awning of a doorway, and then spoke into some kind of walkie-talkie thing.

'Incident on Fifth and 58th Street, assistance required!'

In less than a second, there was the sound of a siren and a police car came zooming around a corner. Two more officers with guns drawn leaped out.

'Where were you attacked?' the first officer asked Megan.

Crouched in the doorway, Megan gaped at them, confused. 'I wasn't attacked.'

'Then what happened?' the officer demanded.

'My wallet was stolen!'

The two newly-arrived policemen looked at each other. Then both lowered their guns and returned to their car. Megan watched as the now silent car moved away at a normal speed. She turned to the officer on the pavement.

'Aren't they going to stay and help you?'

'Help me with what?' he asked. His own gun was now back in its holster.

She came out from the doorway. 'Find the pickpocket who took my wallet!'

Sighing, the officer took out a little notebook. 'Where did the theft happen?'

'I don't know,' Megan said. 'I'm not sure. I was in that store across the street, and I looked in my bag, and it was gone.'

'When was the last time you remember seeing it?' he asked.

Megan thought. 'When I bought some shoes at Barneys. No, wait, I bought the shoes at Bergdorf Goodman. Ohmigod, I can't remember, which one I went to last! I must have the receipt here somewhere.' She began searching through the bags for the slip of paper.

'Maybe you left your wallet in one of those stores.'

Megan shook her head. 'No, no, that's not possible, I'm very careful.'

'Well, I still think it would be worthwhile if you go back and retrace your steps. Ask at the stores if you left your wallet there. The larger stores usually have a "lost and found" department.' He closed his little notebook.

'But . . . I'm telling you, I didn't lose it! It's been stolen! Someone put his hand in my bag and took my wallet.'

'You say "his" hand. Did you see the person?'

'No.'

'Then how do you know the pickpocket was male?'

She was getting very annoyed with this man. Personally, she didn't think he could have been a police officer for very long. He didn't look much older than she was. 'I said "his" hand because I just assumed it was a man. Aren't most pickpockets male?'

'Not necessarily,' he replied. Megan could see he was distracted by a woman who had appeared at his side.

'Could you tell me how to get to the closest subway?'

'Yes, Ma'am, just go up to the next corner, turn right and walk for one block. You'll see the entrance.'

'Thank you,' the woman said and moved on.

Megan tapped her foot impatiently. While this guy was asking her stupid questions and giving directions to other people, the thief was getting further away.

'Officer, what are you going to do about my wallet?' she demanded.

A clear flash of irritation crossed his face before his professional, polite expression returned.

'You can go to the nearest precinct headquarters and fill out a report.'

'And then what?'

'The report will be processed and turned over to the appropriate division, which will begin an investigation.'

'And how long will that take?'

Now the irritation was returning, and he was making no effort to block it. 'I'm really not sure. You can discuss this with someone at the precinct.'

'I don't have time to fill out stupid forms. I'm only here for the weekend.'

He spoke through gritted teeth. 'That's not my problem, Ma'am. Now, if you'll excuse me, I have a job to do.'

'This is your job!' Megan exclaimed. 'I'm the victim of a crime and you're a policeman! You're supposed to help me!'

His eyes were flashing – green eyes. Megan wasn't sure why she was noticing that now. Maybe because they reminded her of traffic lights blinking.

'Ma'am, there are more serious problems than yours in the city of New York!'

'Oh, I see. You can choose which crimes you want to

solve? How nice for you. It's different where I come from, you see. Our police help everyone, regardless of race, religion, sexual orientation . . . or type of crime.'

Her sarcasm appeared to be contagious. The police officer glanced at her bags, the evidence of her shopping, and then gave her a meaningful look. 'It seems to me you might be better off without your wallet.'

Now Megan was furious. 'How dare you! I'm going to report you to your superiors for – for rudeness! And dereliction of duties! I demand to know your name.'

'It's right here, Ma'am.' He indicated the badge on his chest. 'Frank McGuire. Identification number 86392. Here, I'll write it down for you.' The notebook came back out, he wrote on a page and tore it out.

Megan snatched it from his hand. But even in her anger, she was able to remember some manners. 'Thank you,' she snapped.

'Just trying to be co-operative, Ma'am.'

And with a nod, he turned and sauntered away while Megan fumed.

Chapter Ten

Danny had told Erica he wanted to show her the real New York, and that was why they would be taking public transport around town and not cabs. That was fine with Erica, but she found the noise on the crowded subway platform deafening. The passing trains roared so loudly she had to cover her ears.

Things weren't much better when the right train came along and the doors opened. A mass of people poured out, while another mass tried to get in. Danny held onto her arm and pushed them both through with authority. Erica was impressed. Danny was obviously accustomed to taxis, or limos with chauffeurs, but it seemed as though he was just as comfortable with the way ordinary people travelled.

By the time they managed to get on, the carriage was packed with passengers. It seemed like half of them were accompanied by screaming babies or toddlers having tantrums. The other half carried music equipment without the benefit of headphones. There was a man playing an accordion, a woman yelling that the world was about to come to an end, and two barking dogs. Over the din, from some invisible loudspeakers, came muffled announcements. Erica could only hope that none of these announcements applied to her and Danny, since they were totally incomprehensible.

Danny didn't appear to be concerned. It was impossible to talk, but every now and then they exchanged looks and smiled. And they were still holding hands.

Erica didn't really mind that they couldn't talk – they'd been talking non-stop all day, to the point where a guard had to shush them when they visited the Cloisters Museum. At this point in time, she was perfectly content to close her eyes and just enjoy feeling happy.

This day – it was beyond what she'd hoped for. Of course, she had assumed she would like Danny, that he would be a nice person. Months of online conversation had assured her of this. What she'd feared was that he might intimidate her – not intentionally, of course. He was too nice a person to show off and brag about his accomplishments. He probably travelled all over the world on his business trips, but not once had he said anything like 'When I was in Hong Kong' or 'Last week in Sydney'. When he felt a bit peckish, he preferred an ice cream from a street cart to tea at a fancy hotel.

He even told her he'd rather jog in the park than exercise in an expensive health club. 'Too many executive types wanting to talk business when I want to work out,' he'd said.

Danny didn't seem to like talking business at all. Megan and Jennifer were always saying that one of the best ways to flirt was to ask a bloke about his work, to fake an interest even if his work was utterly dull. Erica, who knew very little about money and even less about investments and the stock market, had worried about this. So far, all she'd said was that she was surprised he could take a whole weekday off to spend it with her. 'Oh, the business can run itself,' he'd said casually, and changed the subject. 'There's so much I want to show you.'

Right now, he was taking her to see the Statue of Liberty. They got off the subway at a station called Battery Park, and began walking towards the harbour. She decided to make another effort at demonstrating some interest in his occupation.

'Why did you decide to go into investment work?' she

asked. 'Have you always been keen on the stock market?'

He was silent for a moment, and seemed reluctant to answer. He probably thought it would bore her.

'Really,' she pressed, 'I'm interested.'

'It's kind of personal,' he said. 'But . . .' he paused, and looked at her intently, as if he was trying to make up his mind whether or not he wanted to share something.

'You see, my father played the stock market. I suppose he enjoyed the risk, and he preferred the stock market to casino games or cards. But he really didn't know what he was doing, he didn't understand the market at all. He lost a lot of money, and he didn't have a lot to lose, if you know what I mean. We weren't poor, just ordinary middle class. But with my father's losses, it created hardships.'

Erica had no problem identifying with this. 'My father was into horses. He didn't have an enormous income, and he wasted a lot of it betting. That was one of the reasons my parents divorced. And I know that's why I've never wanted to gamble.'

His eyes lit up. 'That's why my parents broke up too! My mother just got fed up with his crazy investments. She took my brother and me and walked out on him.'

It wasn't a happy story, but it still made her feel good to share this experience with him. The more they talked, the more they discovered they had in common. But one thing puzzled her.

'Then why did you decide to get into the stock market when it was such a disaster for your father?'

'Because I want to help people like my father, to show them how to invest wisely. The stock market isn't a bad thing, but only the very wealthy can afford to play like he did. People need to do their homework. I try to advise them so they won't make mistakes.'

'Did you have to get a special degree to learn how to do this?' she asked him.

He seemed to be weighing his words carefully. 'I'm not really into formal education. I'm pretty much self-taught. I believe you can learn more by doing than studying.'

'That's what I think too,' Erica said. 'I've always wanted to be a chef, but I don't think I need to go to some cooking school to learn how.'

Danny nodded. 'You're probably learning everything you need to know just working at your uncle's restaurant.'

She smiled, but she didn't answer. What could she say? That she could now chop onions twice as fast as she could a year ago? She could use some advice from a successful person, but then she might have to reveal more about her own lack of success. Still, it might be worth it . . .

'But it's happened so fast for you!' she said. 'How were you able to achieve so much so quickly?'

'Just luck, I guess,' he said. 'Hey, you don't really want to talk about work, do you? It's a beautiful day, let's change the subject.'

She was actually relieved. 'OK. Tell me about where we are right now. Because I don't have a clue.'

He grinned. 'We're at the southern tip of Manhattan, close to the waterfront. That's where the ferries leave for the Statue of Liberty and Ellis Island. And if you follow alongside the harbour, you'll come to South Ferry Terminal, where the ferries go to Staten Island.'

They were passing a large, round, metallic sculpture, and Erica paused to admire it.

'That's interesting,' she said. But as she moved closer to it, she frowned. 'It's dented. Is it supposed to be like that? Back in my town, there's a metal sculpture in the park, and it's got dents in it like that. Some idiotic yobs threw rocks at it.'

He didn't respond immediately, and when she looked at him, she was alarmed to see an immense sadness in his face.

'It's called "The Sphere",' he told her. 'It used to be in

the centre of the plaza at the World Trade Center. It's not far from here, you know. The sculpture was recovered after the attacks. That's why it's got some dents and holes.' He pointed, and she looked in that direction. 'That's where the Twin Towers were.'

Erica gazed at the empty space in the sky.

'When the memorial for 9/11 is finished, the sculpture will go back there,' Danny said.

'I remember when it happened,' she said. 'I'd come home early from school, and the TV was on. I thought it was a disaster movie. Where were you?'

'At home. Watching it happen.' He paused. 'Not on TV.'

She gasped. 'You *saw* it?'

'We had a view of the World Trade Center from the roof of our building in Brooklyn. My mother had kept me home from school because I had a dentist's appointment at nine-thirty that morning. We were just getting ready to leave, and we heard about the planes. We went up to the roof, and saw the towers covered in smoke. Then the first one fell . . .' his voice trailed off.

'What did you do?' she asked in a hushed voice.

'I cried,' he said simply. 'I didn't understand what was happening.'

She nodded. 'I can't believe it's been over a decade

since it happened.'

He nodded. 'On the tenth anniversary, there were a lot of speeches and memorial services. I went to one of them. And I cried again, because I still don't understand.'

She could see him as a little boy, holding onto his mother and sobbing. What affected her even more was the image of a grown man, still crying over this horrible and senseless tragedy. Could her feelings for him get any stronger?

When they reached the harbour, Danny told her they had two options. 'We can take the ferry to Liberty Island and go on the tour, but it takes for ever and there's always a line; we'd have to wait an hour or more. I think it's better to take the Staten Island Ferry. You get a good view of the statue from there.'

He was right. The ferry wasn't very crowded, and they positioned themselves at an outside railing, looking over at the distant statue. Once they were moving, Erica felt a chill and shivered. Danny put his arm around her.

'Cold?' he asked.

She smiled. 'Not any more.' So his arm stayed there. And then it felt absolutely right for her to rest her head against his chest. Her heart was so full, she didn't dare speak, and maybe he was feeling the same way because he was silent too. The people around them seemed to fade away. In the back of her mind, Celine Dion was singing. And suddenly, they were Kate Winslett and Leonardo DiCaprio on the *Titanic*.

Instead of an iceberg, the Statue of Liberty rose up before them. She knew it was the symbol of freedom and sanctuary for so many. But for her, it was pure romance. Instinctively, she knew it was time for him to kiss her.

And he did. Another shiver went up her spine, but this one had nothing to do with the cold.

She couldn't remember ever feeling like this before. There had been guys in her life, maybe not recently, but in the not too distant past. She'd liked all of them, some more than others. But now, for the very first time, she believed that she just might be in love.

The ferry trip was over much too soon. But not the feelings. When they disembarked, his arm was still around her, her head was still against his chest. And she was still in love.

Then Danny looked at his watch. 'When do you need to meet your friends?'

'Oh, we haven't made a schedule,' she assured him. 'We're trying not to do everything together.'

'But you'll have dinner with them, won't you?'

The girls hadn't made any definite plans. But maybe the others did expect everyone to meet up back at the hotel. Erica didn't want the others to worry if she didn't show up. On the other hand, she didn't want to leave Danny.

'Would you like to meet the girls?' she asked him. 'We could go back to the hotel and have a drink with them. And then you and I could have dinner alone . . .' Her voice trailed off when she saw the furrows on his brow. Had she gone too far? Was she being pushy?

'I'm really sorry,' he said, 'but I've got something on tonight. A business dinner I can't get out of,' he added quickly.

It seemed a bit odd to her, a business dinner on a Friday night. But then, he'd given her his whole day, and that was something. And maybe he wasn't feeling what she was feeling. Not yet, at least.

'I understand,' she said.

'But we can spend tomorrow together,' he said. 'If you'd like.'

'Yes,' she said. 'I'd like.'

He looked at his watch again, and now he seemed anxious. 'I really have to run. Do you think you can get back to your hotel on your own?'

'Sure, it's not a problem,' she said. 'I've got a map.'

'Would you like me to pick you up at your hotel tomorrow morning?' he asked.

'I have a better idea,' she said. 'I'd like to see where you live. Can I meet you there?'

And again, his eyebrows went up. Mentally, she cursed herself. She *was* being too pushy.

'OK,' he finally said.

She remembered what he'd told her online. 'Park Avenue, right?'

'Yeah.' And he gave her a street number.

'Noon?' she asked. And again she wished she could take back her words. Why couldn't she wait for him to suggest a time?

He nodded. Then he kissed her. It felt a little different this time – too light, too rushed. And then he was gone, leaving a confused Erica behind.

Chapter Eleven

Two hours after her confrontation with Officer Frank McGuire, NYPD, Megan was still fuming. Pacing the hotel suite, she tried to decide what she could do with her anger.

She had called her bank in the UK and informed them of the theft, so she wouldn't be liable for any charges made on the credit card, or any money withdrawn. According to the efficient person she'd spoken to, new cards would arrive at her hotel tomorrow, so she could still do a little more shopping before she left New York. That was good news.

She'd also discovered some loose bills at the bottom of her handbag, which would tide her over till she could borrow money from one of her friends. She knew she should be feeling relieved. But all she could think about was that obnoxious, nasty, unbelievably rude policeman who had refused to help her, who had pretty much insulted her. How dare he treat her like that! At home, she would have been treated with courtesy and sympathy. Could it be so different here? Surely, this wasn't the way American policemen were trained to behave. Officer Frank McGuire had to be an exception. His superiors should know about his obnoxious conduct. And Megan decided that they would.

She left the suite, took the lift down to the lobby and went to reception. Nick was still at the desk.

'Hi, what can I do for you?' he asked with his professional smile firmly in place.

'I need to know the address of the police station closest to Madison Avenue and 68th Street.'

The smile disappeared. 'Is there a problem?' Then his eyes widened and he looked *seriously* concerned. 'It's not Jennifer, is it? Was she picked up for stalking a celebrity?'

Megan raised an eyebrow.

'Not to my knowledge,' she told him. 'Not yet, at least. My wallet was stolen somewhere around that location.'

Nick expressed his sympathy for her plight, checked his computer and gave her an address.

She had no difficulty locating the station. Figuring out where to go once she was inside was the problem. Megan had never been in a police station before, and she had no idea if the chaotic environment was normal.

'Pardon me,' she said to a uniformed woman, but she was ignored. When she saw that the woman was escorting a handcuffed man, she stopped trying to get her attention. On a bench, an elderly woman was wailing. Two boys who couldn't have been more than thirteen were swearing loudly. And two heavily made-up young women, both in skin-tight, ultra-short miniskirts and tiny halter tops were giggling. Megan wondered whether they were criminals or victims.

There was a complete absence of directional signs or indications of where one should go to file a complaint about a police officer. And no one approached her to ask if she needed help. Finally, she located a long counter which looked like some sort of reception desk, and she joined the queue of people waiting to be seen by one bored-looking uniformed man, who wasn't being very pleasant to the people seeking his assistance. She couldn't hear very well with all the noise going on around her, but she could see that each person who approached him barely got a few words out before he snarled at them and sent them off.

When it was finally her turn, she decided to turn on the charm in the hope that it might produce a better response from him. Smiling brightly, she said, 'Pardon me, sir, I do hope you can help me, I have a special problem. You see, my wallet was taken by a pickpocket, and—'

'Third floor, second door on the right, stolen goods,' he said. 'Next.'

But Megan didn't budge. 'No, wait! I also want to enter an official complaint about the treatment I received from one of your men. When I asked him if—'

Once again, he wouldn't let her finish. 'Third floor, first door on left, complaints department. Next!'

She wanted to hold her ground and make him listen, but the woman behind her had other ideas. Megan experienced a sharp jab to the ribs, which shoved her out of the line.

'How dare you!' Megan exclaimed. 'Could I get some help here, please? That woman pushed me!'

No one came to her aid. Now she had *three* complaints to file. A stolen wallet, a bad cop and an assault.

On the third floor, she went to the first door on the left. There was a queue here, too, but it moved much faster. When it was her turn at the desk, she realised why.

'I'd like to make a complaint about one of your officers,' she began, and that was as far as she got. The woman behind the counter handed her a form and said, 'Next!'

Megan didn't want to risk another elbow in her ribs, so she moved aside and looked at the form. Tiny print covered both sides and she had to squint to read it. It turned out to be a very long series of questions which demanded details as to the precise nature of her complaint.

Outside in the hall, there was a row of student-style desk chairs which she assumed were for the use of people filling out forms. Naturally, all were occupied. After about ten minutes, one became free and she grabbed it. But then she discovered she had neither a pen nor a pencil in her bag, and by the time she'd got up and found one her chair had been taken.

After waiting another ten minutes, Megan decided that this was ridiculous, and she could fill out the form in the comfort of her hotel suite and bring it back.

By now Megan was in an extremely bad mood. So when she spotted her arch-nemesis Officer Frank McGuire coming up the steps as she was going down, she decided it was time to give him what for. OK, maybe the thief who stole her wallet was the number one villain, but this policeman was a close second, and unlike the pickpocket, he was *there*.

She thought he'd take off when he saw her coming towards him, but he actually stopped and made no effort to escape. This was surprising, considering that he had to have noticed the look of fury on her face. But then, maybe he didn't remember their encounter. He'd probably helped – or *refused* to help – a hundred other victims since they met.

But Frank McGuire seemed to know exactly who Megan was.

'Did you report your missing wallet?' he asked.

'Not missing,' she said crisply. 'Stolen.'

He nodded. 'OK, did you report your *stolen* wallet?'

'No. I was visiting the complaints department. To complain about *you*.'

She rather hoped he'd turn pale, or at least look a little nervous when he learned this. He only nodded.

'Feel better now?' he asked.

'I'll feel a lot better when I know you've lost your job!' she snapped. 'You have no business being a police officer.'

He still didn't seem alarmed. 'Look, Miss . . . Miss . . .'

'Briggs. Megan Briggs.'

'Look, Miss Briggs, I don't know what things are like where you come from – where *do* you come from?'

'England.'

'London?'

'No, a town you've never heard of. And what difference does that make anyway?'

'This is Manhattan, Miss Briggs. It's a very big city and there's a lot of crime, serious crime. The kind of crimes where people get hurt. Crimes that take precedence over the theft of a wallet.'

She was on the verge of telling him that she was very much aware of this, that she'd just been practically attacked in the police station, but for some reason she held her tongue. Maybe it had something to do with the sudden intensity she saw in his face.

'I know it was upsetting to you, losing your wallet.' He held up his hand to ward off any objection. 'Or having it stolen. And stealing *is* a crime in New York, just like everywhere in the United States. But unfortunately, there just aren't enough police officers to go chasing after a pickpocket, especially when the victim can't describe the perpetrator or even state precisely where the theft took place. There's always a chance that the thief will get caught if he tries to use your credit card in a store. But your average pickpocket knows better. He'll take out the cash and toss the wallet in a trash can. Maybe someone else will find the wallet and turn it in.'

Megan stared at him incredulously. 'Are you saying that this is normal? That there's nothing the police will do about a stolen wallet?'

He was beginning to look a little irritated. 'Miss Briggs, what do you want the police to do? Search all the trash bins on the Upper East Side of New York?'

'Actually, it might have been stolen before I came uptown,' Megan said.

He threw up his hands. 'Do you have any idea how many trash cans there are in New York? Look, I'm sorry about your wallet. But we've got bigger fish to fry! Let me tell you something. I'm twenty-two years old, I just graduated from the Police Academy. I've been on the job for three months. And I've already been involved in a murder, two cases of arson and a drive-by shooting in which an innocent child was wounded. There are people in this city with real problems!'

'My problems are real too!' Megan exclaimed.

'You know what I think your problem is?' Frank McGuire asked. He didn't wait for her to respond. 'I think you're a spoiled princess whose shopping excursion was interrupted. I think you honestly believe you're the centre of the universe and no one else matters as much as you do. And I'll tell you right now, if action is taken on your complaint about me, all that will happen is that I'll get a reprimand. And you know what? It will be totally worth it, just to have had the opportunity to tell you what you are!' With that, he turned and continued up the stairs.

Megan wasn't sure how long she continued to stand there with her mouth open. It wasn't until a couple of passers by glanced at her oddly that she realised she must look a little strange. Well, why wouldn't she? She was shocked, angry, stunned by this attack on her character. She was feeling something else too, though she couldn't quite put her finger on it.

Suddenly, she felt an enormous need to be with people who cared about her, who knew her, who didn't think she was some kind of spoiled princess. She needed her mates. Of course, Erica probably wanted to spend all her time with her online boyfriend. But Megan would be willing to join Serena and go to some boring cultural event, or even accompany Jennifer on a celebrity hunt. She just wanted to be with friends.

To her surprise, she found Erica back in their suite. She was sitting on the sofa in front of the TV, remote in hand, and staring at the screen.

'What are *you* doing here? I thought you'd be out with your guy!' Then she lowered her voice. 'Is he here?'

'No,' Erica said. 'I *was* with him. But now I'm not.'

'I don't understand. Weren't you going to spend the day with him?'

'I did,' Erica said glumly. 'The day is over.'

'Oh, dear,' Megan said, sitting down next to her. 'Was he awful?'

'No. He was wonderful.'

Megan frowned. 'Then I don't get it.'

'Neither do I,' Erica sighed. 'We were having such a good time. He took me to a trendy restaurant where we had a gorgeous lunch, and then we walked all over the city. Everything was fine, we got along beautifully. Then, out of the blue, he tells me he has plans for the evening. *Business* plans. Who has business plans on a Friday night?'

Megan tried to be helpful. 'Important businessmen?'

'But he told me he'd rearranged his work so he could spend the day with me. He even said the business could run itself.' She bit her lower lip. 'Maybe he didn't find me quite as wonderful as I found him. Maybe he was sick of me.'

'Did he *act* like he was tired of being with you? Did he seem bored?'

'No.'

'Then I'm sure he wasn't,' Megan stated firmly. 'Boys are terrible actors, they can't hide their feelings. He just had some sort of engagement he couldn't get out of, that's all.'

'Yeah, but what kind of engagement?' Erica wondered. 'It might not have been business at all.'

'Do you think he could be involved with someone?' Megan asked.

Erica shrugged. 'Who knows?'

Megan had another idea. 'You don't think he could be married, do you?'

Erica looked stricken for a moment, then shook her head. 'We're meeting at his apartment tomorrow morning. He wouldn't let me come there if he was married. Even if the wife wasn't at home, there'd be evidence of her, right?'

'True,' Megan agreed hesitantly.

Erica sighed. 'But I do get this feeling there's something he's not telling me.'

Megan shook her head. 'Good grief, Erica. You've spent one day with him, you couldn't have learned every detail of his life. And we all have secrets.'

'I suppose,' Erica murmured. 'How was your day?'

Megan told her about the loss of her wallet and her experience with one of New York's finest. Erica was appropriately sympathetic.

'How dreadful for you! And that cop sounds like a very nasty character.'

'And he was utterly useless,' Megan went on. 'He did

absolutely nothing, he completely refused to help me.'

Erica looked thoughtful. 'Did you see the pickpocket who took your wallet?'

Megan shook her head. 'I'm not even sure when and where it happened.'

'Then there really wasn't much the policeman could do, was there?'

Megan was annoyed. 'Are you taking his side?'

'No, of course not! Even if he couldn't do anything, he should have been nicer to you.'

'Actually . . . he was OK at first. But when I started asking questions, he got a bit stroppy . . .' In her mind, she recalled the encounter.

'He was very young,' she said suddenly. 'Not much older than us.'

'What does that have to do with anything?' Erica asked. 'It's no excuse for bad behaviour.'

Megan shrugged. 'I don't know. Maybe he hasn't been a cop very long and he doesn't have very much experience dealing with people,' she said, unconvincingly.

'I'm sure that's all it was,' Erica said. 'He must be like that with everyone. It wasn't personal.'

'But he *was* personal!' Megan cried out. ' "Erica, he called me a spoiled princess!'

Erica gazed at her curiously.

'Why are you looking at me like that?' Megan said, defensively.

'I'm starting to think you're more upset about that police officer than losing your wallet.'

Megan tossed her head. 'That's nonsense.' She took the remote control from Erica and pressed the channel button. 'Look, it's *Babes in Manhattan*.'

Erica glanced at the screen. 'It's a repeat. Megan . . . what did this policeman look like?'

A clear mental picture of Officer Frank McGuire materialised. 'He's about six feet tall, maybe a little more. Broad shoulders. Dark blond hair, short. Nice teeth.'

'Eyes?'

'Green. Mossy green, set wide apart.'

'Cute?'

Megan looked at her sharply. 'What are you getting at?'

Erica grinned. 'I'm just wondering, if some old, balding, police officer called you a spoiled princess, would you be so upset?'

'Don't talk rubbish,' Megan said. But in her mind, she saw those green eyes and she couldn't help wondering what they might look like if the guy hadn't been so angry.

She forced herself to pay attention to the programme on the television. 'Oh, I remember this one. It was just after Tori caught her boyfriend cheating on her and the girls took her to a club.'

'And they danced all night and flirted with strangers,' Erica continued. 'And Tori lost her shoes.'

'Which is exactly what we should do,' Megan declared.

'What? Lose our shoes?'

'No, go out dancing and flirt with strangers.' Megan got up and went to the little desk. 'Weren't there some passes to a trendy club among that stuff the TV people left for us?' She rifled through the papers. 'Yes, here it is, it's a place called the Cottage. We just have to show this to the person at the door and he'll let us in. We even get a free drink each.' She tucked the paper in her bag. 'Come on, girlfriend, let's put on something sexy and fabulous. We'll get a bite to eat, and then we'll go have a wild night on the town. You'll forget all about your tycoon.'

Erica jumped up. 'And you can forget about your policeman.'

Megan made a dismissive gesture. 'Easy-peasy,' she said with as much nonchalance as she could muster. 'I don't even need the club for that, I've already forgotten all about it.' But something about the knowing expression in Erica's eyes told her she hadn't sounded very convincing.

Chapter Twelve

Still clutching her shopping bags, Serena checked her watch as the lift went up to the sixth floor. It was almost seven o'clock. She had just enough time to change into her new clothes and pick up a sandwich to eat on her way to Lincoln Center. For the moment, she wasn't even thinking about her lost suitcase. She was giddy with excitement about the evening ahead.

She found two of her roomies all dressed up and preening in front of a mirror.

'What are you up to?' she asked.

'We're going out dancing,' Erica told her.

'That's nice. Is your online boyfriend going with you?'

'No, he has to work tonight. But we had a great day together, and I'm seeing him tomorrow. How do we look?'

Serena cocked her head thoughtfully as she took

in their outfits. Megan wore tight leopard-skin leggings and a low-cut black tunic. Erica was decked out in a black leather miniskirt and a tiny tee that didn't even reach her waist.

'Like you're going dancing.'

'Want to come?' Erica asked.

'No, thanks, I've got plans,' Serena said. 'I'm so excited! I got the last ticket for tonight's production.'

'A broadway show?' Erica asked.

'No, it's a new opera. I saw the newspaper reviews when it played in London last week. It's supposed to be phenomenal!'

'A phenomenal opera,' Megan murmured. She shook her head in disbelief. 'Does such a thing really exist? A bunch of fat people singing in a language no one understands. What a thrill.'

Serena laughed good-naturedly. She was used to the girls poking fun at her taste in entertainment. 'Oh, don't be such a philistine. First off, opera singers aren't necessarily fat. And this is a modern opera, in English. Actually, it's quite controversial.'

'Why?' Erica asked. 'Is it performed in the nude?'

'*No*. It's a modern interpretation of Mozart's *The Marriage of Figaro*, with some new music added and some variations in the plot. People think it's heresy to meddle with Mozart, but personally, I'm very curious.' She went into the bedroom and emptied her bags on the bed. With the door open, she could still hear the girls in the sitting room.

'Do you have any idea what she's talking about?' Megan asked Erica.

'Well, I've heard of Mozart,' Erica replied. 'Who's Figaro?'

As she changed in the bedroom, Serena called out an explanation.

'He was the barber of Seville, and now he's the chief servant of the Count. The Count's married, but now he wants this girl Susanna, who's engaged to Figaro. Then there's this other woman who's in love with Figaro, and this pageboy who's in love with the daughter of the Count's gardener, and everyone's sneaking around and hiding and disguising themselves to get together.'

'Sounds confusing to me,' Megan commented.

'It's not, it's funny,' Serena said, emerging from the bedroom. She modelled her new clothes for the others. 'How do I look?'

Erica grinned. 'Like you're going to an opera.'

'For your information, people don't wear leopard-skin leggings and leather miniskirts to the opera,' Serena retorted. She blew them kisses and hurried out of the door. Waiting for the lift, she smiled as she thought about her friends. She knew they weren't impressed with her attire, and she wouldn't be caught dead in either of the outfits they were wearing. But at least they all they accepted each other the way they were, and that's what kept their friendships going.

The doors to the lift opened, and Jennifer stepped out.

'Serena, hello, my dear!' she shrieked. 'What are you doing tonight?'

'Going to the opera,' Serena said, noting her friend's overexcited demeanour. 'How about you?'

'Got a date with Jordan Blake,' Jennifer announced. 'Sort of. Have fun!' She ran down the hall towards their room.

'You too,' Serena called after her. So Jennifer's celebrity dreams were coming true. Everything was working out for everybody. If all this good luck continued, maybe she'd even get her suitcase back before the weekend was over.

Serena had seen photos of the famous Lincoln Center for the Performing Arts, but nothing could have prepared her for its magnificence. Among its various venues was the Metropolitan Opera House, home to the New York City Ballet and the Philharmonic Orchestra, as well as the opera. On the plaza in front of the building was a huge fountain with cascading water, and the lights from the Met's interior cast a golden glow over it.

The opera house itself, with its deep red seating and enormous crystal chandeliers, was breathtaking. Her seat was in one of the balconies, far from the stage but with an excellent view.

She opened the programme and read about the production. It seemed that the story was essentially the same, with a lot of hiding and disguising and mistaken identities, but modernised. She was about to look at the page that listed the performers, to see if she recognized the names of any renowned opera singers, but she was prevented by the dimming of the lights. Closing the programme, she watched in awe as the huge chandeliers rose up to the ceiling. And then the curtain went up.

From the beginning, she was entranced. She'd only seen a production of the traditional opera on the telly, and she'd never seen a professional live performance of any opera. With the characters in contemporary dress and the words in English, this version was lively and even funnier than Serena had imagined it would be. Some of the music had been reworked to a modern beat, and she could see how it was controversial – you weren't supposed to mess around with Mozart! But the voices were incredible, and she was enjoying every minute of it. She particularly liked the character of Cherubino, the Count's pageboy, who was played by a jolly, sturdy young man with curly dark hair who sang like a dream and even looked like a mischief-maker, which was how Serena had envisioned the character.

Cherubino had a beautiful aria in Act One, but it was in Act Two that he really got to demonstrate his acting ability. This was the scene where he was going to disguise himself as Susanna, the bride-to-be of Figaro, in an effort to trick the Count. When the husky young man emerged from a closet in a sparkling green gown, the audience erupted in laughter. Serena opened her mouth to join in the reaction, but her laughter turned to a gasp.

She knew that gown, she'd seen it before. In the suitcase she'd brought home from the airport.

A coincidence? She might have accepted it until Cherubino appeared again in the next scene, still disguised, but in a different dress. Another gown that she recognised. That one had been in the suitcase too.

Now, as much as she was enjoying the show, she couldn't wait for the intermission. And as soon as the lights went up, she grabbed the programme and, turning to the cast list, found the name of the singer portraying Cherubino. Then she sank back in her seat.

There it was, the Feldman she'd been searching for. With a first name she would have completely disregarded in the directory listings.

Joseph.

Chapter Thirteen

Jennifer tried very hard to appear blasé and nonchalant, as if she went to the concerts of famous rock stars every day. She'd seen enough films of concerts to know what to wear, and she knew she looked good in the short, tight leather skirt and fabulous shiny patent leather boots that went all the way up to her thighs. She'd teased her blonde hair out to a wild mane, and with her dark, smoky eyes and pale-pink frosted lipstick, she knew she'd fit in and still stand out.

But it wasn't easy, pretending to be indifferent once she got her first look at the inside of Madison Square Garden.

'Ohmigod,' she murmured.

Nick appreciated her reaction. 'This is one of the largest arenas in the world,' he told her. 'A lot of major sporting events are held here. And big concerts, of course. Michael Jackson, Elton John, Lady Gaga – they've all played the Garden.'

Jennifer was wide-eyed as she took in the crowds pouring into the arena. 'I've never in my life seen so many people in one place.'

'It seats around 20,000,' Nick told her. 'And it's sold out tonight.'

She was giddy with excitement. 'Where are our seats?'

Nick checked the tickets. 'On the loge level. That's the first balcony.'

Jennifer's face fell slightly. 'Oh. I thought maybe we'd be on the floor. In the first row. After all, you did Jordan Blake a big favour.'

Nick laughed. 'Dragging you out of his suite? It was a pleasure. And for your information, these are going to be great seats.' They started up the stairs to the loge, and when they reached their seats, she had to admit he knew what he was talking about.

'Great view, right?' he asked. 'You can see the whole stage; there's nothing blocking it.'

'Yeah,' she said.

He seemed puzzled by her lack of enthusiasm, and then his expression cleared. 'Oh, I get it. You want Jordan Blake to be able to see *you*.'

Jennifer nodded. 'I've heard that sometimes he picks a

girl from the audience to dance with him onstage. He's not going to choose someone way up in a balcony.'

Nick nodded seriously. 'Ah, I understand. That sounds like something my sister would say.'

'You see, I'm not that unusual,' she said.

'Not at all,' Nick replied. 'Only my sister is twelve.'

Jennifer sighed. She might as well speak honestly. After all, it wasn't as if she needed to impress *him*. 'OK, maybe I seem a little silly to you. But all this . . .' she waved her hand towards the stage, 'this is probably no big deal to you. You have to understand that my life back home is exceedingly boring, there's never any excitement at all. I live in a boring bedsit, I take boring classes, I go out with boring blokes to boring places.'

'Oh, come on,' Nick remonstrated. 'It can't be that bad. If you really hated your life, you'd be depressed. And you don't seem like a depressed person.'

This was true. She wasn't depressed, mainly because she'd always accepted her life as normal, not terrible. But she wanted more! She tried to explain.

'This trip to New York, it's my big chance to see exciting people, to get close to them. And I'm not going to miss any opportunity.'

She steeled herself for his reaction to this confession. Was he going to laugh at her?

He didn't. He actually seemed intrigued. 'But why are you so interested in celebrities?'

'Because . . . because they live fabulous lives. And I want to know what that's like, to be fabulous, and glamorous, and do exciting things.'

'Do you really think getting close to a celebrity would completely change your life?'

'No . . . but it would make my life more interesting.' She looked at Nick thoughtfully. 'You must see celebrities all the time at your hotel.'

'They come and they go,' he admitted. 'We get our fair share.'

'Who have you seen?'

He offered up a few names that made her catch her breath.

'Wow! How do you keep your mind on your work when people like that are standing right in front of you?'

'They're just people, Jennifer. Some are nice, some are nasty. Some are . . .' he stopped and grinned.

'What's so funny?' she asked.

'I was just remembering one of them. I'm not going to tell you his name, but he was a big tennis star. He was playing a grand slam tournament here, and he lost big time. The press was all over the place, surrounding the hotel, and he wanted to get back to his room without seeing any of them. So he called me from his car, to see if I could help out.'

'Did you help him?'

His eyes sparkled as he recalled the incident. 'We've got a lost-and-found closet behind the reception area. A recent family from Saudi Arabia had just checked out, and the woman had left a burqa in the closet. You know, the Muslim gown that completely covers the woman except for her eyes.'

Jennifer nodded.

'So I took the burqa and met the tennis player around the corner from the hotel. He put it on in the car, and walked right into the hotel without anyone paying any attention to him at all.' He grinned. 'Fortunately, nobody noticed the sneakers on his feet.'

Jennifer burst out laughing. This guy might just be serving as an excuse to get closer to Jordan, but she was enjoying herself immensely with him. Too bad Nick wasn't a celebrity.

Encouraged by her appreciation, Nick told her more stories – about the wealthy tycoon who stole every moveable object from his room, the opera singer who practised her arias in the lift because she liked the way her voice sounded there . . . Jennifer could have listened to these stories all night, but suddenly the lights dimmed and an unseen voice declared, 'Ladies and gentlemen, Jordan Blake!'

Screams went up from the crowd, and Jennifer thought she could hear her own over all the others. And there he was, the greatest pop idol since . . . who? Michael Jackson? Elvis? All four Beatles?

He went straight into his current hit, and the audience went berserk. But the Garden had an amazing sound system, and Jennifer could actually hear him over the roar of the crowd.

She owned all his albums, and she listened to him a lot on her iPod. But hearing him like this was a whole new experience. Within ten minutes, he had the entire audience on its feet, jumping up and down, waving their hands in the air, trying to dance without any dancing space. Jennifer had never tried any drugs, she didn't drink heavily, but for once she thought she knew what it felt like to be high.

But it was the romantic songs that really got to her. His voice sent shivers up and down her spine. And it wasn't just the voice, it was the emotion he put into the words he sang. She felt like he was singing directly to her, even though everyone else in the audience must be having the same experience.

She'd heard the songs so many times, but had she ever really listened to the words? She heard them now.

> *I see you, shining, like the only star in the sky,*
> *I always know when you are near,*
> *I'm waiting, and I'm searching,*
> *But where are you, my one and only love?*
> *And will I ever find you . . .*

I'm here, Jordan, I'm right here, she wanted to tell him. I'm waiting for you too. There was so much feeling in those words, she felt absolutely certain that they must be true, that he hadn't yet found his one, true love. And why couldn't that true love be Jennifer Hawkins? She had to meet him, she absolutely had to get his attention. Maybe Nick was able to prevent this in the hotel, but he wasn't the boss of Madison Square Garden. He couldn't stop her here.

She didn't want the concert to end, but at the same time, she couldn't wait for it to end. She had a plan. The cheers and applause brought him back for three encores, and he deserved it, but she was beginning to fidget. Finally, despite the continuing applause, he didn't come back onto the stage and the lights went up.

She turned to Nick. 'I don't suppose the tickets you

got came with backstage passes, did they?'

'Sorry, no.'

'Doesn't matter,' she said. 'I'm going backstage.'

'Are you nuts?' he asked. 'You'll never get in!'

She grinned. 'I *told* you, I'm not passing up any opportunity.' And with that, she moved out to the aisle and joined the masses leaving the arena. With a little pushing, squeezing and ignoring cries of protest, she managed to get out of the arena and into the huge entrance hall. Once she was outside, she began circling the building in search of an entrance to the backstage area.

She found it – but not before at least a hundred other fans found it first. That didn't put her off. Once again, she pushed and squeezed, and eventually found herself in front of a door, which was guarded by half a dozen big men wearing special badges. Bodyguards, she presumed.

A woman and a man, both of whom wore strings around their necks with laminated labels attached, approached the door. One of the big men checked the labels, and pushed people aside to let the couple in. Jennifer tried to follow them, but the big man blocked her.

She moved away and poked another guard. 'Excuse

me, I'm supposed to go backstage.'

'Name?' he barked.

'Jennifer Hawkins.'

He looked at a clipboard. 'You're not on the list.'

'Oh, there must be a mistake. Jordan and I are staying at the same hotel, we met this morning, he invited me to come backstage after the concert. He's expecting me.'

The man shook his head. 'If you don't have an all access pass and you're not on the list, you're not getting in.'

'How can I get a pass?' she asked. But the guard ignored her, and another guard began pushing her back into the crowd. Looking around, Jennifer could see that most of them were much younger, and many were carrying what looked like autograph books. Ordinary fans. She didn't want Jordan coming out and seeing her with *them*.

Discouraged, she moved away from the crowd. Somehow, she'd have to find him in the hotel. Nick wouldn't be working at the desk tonight. Maybe Jordan would bring his entourage back to the hotel to party . . .

'Jennifer!'

She turned to see Nick, standing by the curb. She didn't particularly want to hear him say 'I told you so' but at least he'd take her back to the hotel. He was smiling as she approached, but it wasn't a mocking smile. It was almost sympathetic.

'No luck, huh?' he asked.

Jennifer affected a nonchalant air. 'It's just too crowded, I can't be bothered.'

'You know, a lot of these rock 'n' roll types hit the clubs after a concert,' he told her.

'I know,' she said. 'Places like the Cottage.'

He raised his eyebrows. 'You know about the Cottage?'

'Oh sure, I read about it all the time in magazines,' she told him. She could see the photos in her head – people like Brad and Angelina being ushered beyond the velvet rope by a burly bouncer who kept all the riff-raff out. 'It's the trendiest club in New York, right?'

'Absolutely,' Nick replied. 'A lot of celebrities go there.'

Jennifer sighed. 'And it's really exclusive. You pretty much have to *be* a celebrity to get in.'

'Not if you know the bouncer,' Nick said.

Jennifer's mouth fell open. 'You know the bouncer? Are you saying I could get in?'

'If you're with me,' he replied with a smile.

This bloke was full of surprises, Jennifer thought. Happily, she linked her arm with his as he hailed a taxi.

He told her more celebrity stories on the way to the club, about the most handsome movie star in the world who had unspeakably bad breath; the notable conservative politician who threw wild parties; and the young teen singer with a squeaky clean image who had to be rushed to hospital after a drinking binge. The club was way downtown, and there was a lot of traffic, but he kept her entertained all the way. He certainly had an interesting job, she thought. But she couldn't help wondering what his life was like outside of the hotel. Nick was quite a good-looking guy himself – not a Jordan Blake, of course, but definitely attractive. He was funny too, and clearly intelligent . . .

As he finished one of his stories, she was about to ask him a question about himself when the car pulled up to a curb. 'Wanna get out here?' the driver asked. 'We'll be stuck in a line of cars letting people out if I try to get any closer.'

'Sure,' Nick said, and he paid the driver. As they got out of the taxi, Jennifer looked around apprehensively. This didn't look like the kind of neighbourhood that the rich and famous would frequent. The street was dark and deserted and the buildings looked dilapidated.

Nick must have sensed her concern. 'Don't worry,' he assured her. 'It's not as bad as it looks.'

She didn't want him thinking she was a hick. 'I'm not

worried,' she said quickly. But she didn't object when he took her hand.

Right around the corner, the neighbourhood was still run-down, but it wasn't deserted. A long line of people stood waiting on the pavement, and there was a queue of taxis and limousines letting people out in front of a door cordoned off with a velvet rope. And there stood yet another big man with a clipboard.

This one looked even scarier than the guards back at the concert. He had huge broad shoulders, tattoos running up and down his bare arms and a fierce face. But when Nick approached, the man's expression changed. He broke into a big smile and embraced the receptionist.

'Yo, bro! What's happening?' he barked.

'Not much, my man,' Nick replied.

The big guy unhooked the velvet rope and ushered them in. Jennifer could hear the groans and complaints from the people in line behind them. She almost felt like a celebrity herself.

Inside, the lights were dim, and the music was thumping. The place might have been called the Cottage, but it certainly bore no resemblance to any cottage Jennifer had ever seen. Everything was black and gold. There were banquettes with gold and black zebra stripes, shiny black tables with gold stools and huge golden chandeliers that hung from a black ceiling. A dance floor was lit with golden lights coming from beneath the smoked glass floor. Beautiful people were three-deep around a bar that encircled the large room, and above the dance floor was a balcony where a DJ provided the music.

Jennifer was ecstatic. It was exactly like the pictures she'd seen. This was the kind of place Jordan would frequent, and even if he didn't come in tonight, there were bound to be other celebs for her to encounter.

'Hey, guess who's here!' Nick exclaimed.

Jennifer clutched his arm. 'Who? Where?'

'Your friends! Over there, look!'

Jennifer followed his gaze and saw Erica and Megan, sitting on stools at one of the high tables. With mixed emotions, she accompanied Nick in their direction. She smiled, pleased to see the girls, but she would have preferred Nick to have pointed out Paris Hilton or someone like that.

Her friends looked surprised and pleased to see them.

'Having fun?' Nick asked.

They both nodded, but Jennifer detected a certain lack of enthusiasm in their faces. Erica seemed more interested in her tall glass with mint leaves hanging over the edge.

'What's that?' Jennifer asked.

'Mojito,' Erica replied.

'Her third,' Megan pointed out, and took a ladylike sip from her glass of wine.

'Better be careful,' Nick said to Erica. 'Those are pretty strong drinks.'

'We came here to forget our problems,' Megan told Nick, 'and Erica needs help to do that.'

'What kind of problems?' Nick asked.

'Man problems,' Erica muttered.

'Sorry to hear that,' Nick said. 'I apologise for my gender.'

Jennifer giggled. Nick could be so witty. But her smile faded as Megan told Nick about the online boyfriend who had blown off Erica for the evening. She'd heard the story already, back in the hotel, but she felt more sympathy now than she had when she'd first heard about Erica's plight. Erica was really down. And she was drinking that mojito really fast. Way too fast.

'I just don't get it,' Erica mumbled. 'We had a wonderful day together, we got along beautifully.'

'Are you talking about the guy who sent you the

flowers?' Nick asked. He looked almost upset Jennifer noticed.

Erica nodded. 'I thought we were having such a good time, we were truly connecting. And then he suddenly had other plans for the evening! He blew me off.' She wiped her eye. 'I guess he's just not that into me.'

'Hey, don't jump to conclusions,' Nick warned her. 'There's probably a rational explanation.' Are you going to see him again?'

Erica nodded. 'He said he'd meet me tomorrow.'

Nick looked relieved. 'There you go. He wouldn't want to see you again if he wasn't into you.'

Now Erica was sniffling, and her voice was even more slurred. 'Then why isn't he with me tonight? Whatever other plans he had, he could have gotten out of them if he really cared about me.'

Nick seemed to be struggling for an explanation. 'Maybe . . . maybe he just didn't want to seem too forthright – or eager?'

'Yes, that's it!' Jennifer chimed in. 'He thought he'd seem too pushy if he insisted you stay together tonight. He was afraid that would turn you off.' She put an arm around Erica. 'Listen to Nick, he's a man, he knows how guys think.'

Now the tears were streaming down Erica's face. 'I

really like him, Jen. I think I could love him.'

'Oh, stop it, Erica,' Megan said. 'You just met him today!'

'Megan!' Jennifer said fiercely. 'Erica's really upset.' Erica was sobbing now, with her head on Jennifer's shoulder.

Megan, who was never very comfortable with public displays of emotion, tried to distract everyone. 'Who's that guy over by the bar? He looks so familiar.'

Nick looked. 'I think it's Ashton Kutcher. Hey, Jennifer, there's a celebrity by the bar!'

Jennifer frowned at him and shook her head. Like she'd ever leave a weeping friend!

'Nick, I can't leave Erica. She's upset.'

Nick didn't look disturbed by her lack of interest. In fact, his smile grew even warmer.

Chapter Fourteen

Excited and more than a little nervous, Serena joined the throngs leaving Lincoln Center, but she didn't continue on with them to where the taxis were waiting. She cut away from the crowd and began walking around the Met in search of a stage door entrance.

She figured she wouldn't have any trouble finding it. There had to be hordes of people waiting for the cast to emerge, so they could get autographs and take photos. What if she couldn't get close enough to Joseph Feldman to explain why she was there? But it turned out that opera lovers weren't like the fans of rock stars. She found a door clearly marked 'Stage', and the area was deserted. There were no guards, no fans, nothing to suggest that important people would be coming out.

She checked her watch. He couldn't have left yet. It would take him a while to get out of his costume and take off his make-up. She wondered if she would even recognise him without it. Even in the scenes where he had appeared as a man, his dark curly hair could have been a wig.

The stage door opened and she held her breath. Three women emerged, all complaining about the conductor. The next person to emerge was a man she recognised as the Count. More and more people came out, and Serena got more and more nervous. What if he was hidden from view by other performers? What if he moved too quickly for her to stop him? What if—

And then, there he was, with real dark curly hair and the same jaunty step as Cherubino. Only he was much younger than she thought he would be. Not too tall, and a little stocky, but with a face that was a lot cuter without all the stage make-up. Quickly, she stepped towards him.

'Excuse me, are you Cherubino?' She couldn't believe she'd just said that. 'I mean, Joseph Feldman?'

He stopped. 'That depends. Are you a fan or a mugger?'

'Neither,' Serena said. 'I mean, I'm a fan, I loved your performance tonight, it was a magnificent production and you were wonderful, absolutely wonderful, I was ever so impressed . . .' Even as the words left her mouth, she knew she was blathering on like an idiot and he must think she was crazy. 'I'm sorry, I'll stop now.'

He was grinning. 'Hey, don't stop on my account. I can handle compliments.'

She took a deep breath. 'What I'm trying to say is that even though I enjoyed your performance enormously, that's not why I'm here. It's about a suitcase.'

'A suitcase,' he repeated. Then his eyebrows shot up. 'My suitcase?'

'And mine,' she said. 'You see, I flew in from Heathrow yesterday, and I picked up the wrong suitcase. When I saw your costumes on stage tonight, I recognised them. Did you by any chance arrive from the UK yesterday and pick up mine?'

'Did your suitcase, by any chance, just happen to contain an enormous book called *Spiritual Motifs in Art of the High Renaissance*?'

She nodded excitedly.

'You know, when I was dragging that suitcase through the airport, I *thought* it seemed unusually heavy,' the singer said. 'But I just chalked it up to being exhausted and jet-lagged. And then when I opened the bag at home, I went into a total panic. Fortunately, the Met has duplicates of all the costumes.'

'Good,' Serena said. 'Unfortunately, my hotel didn't

have duplicates of my clothes.'

'Then you need your bag, and the Met will be happy when I can produce the costumes,' he said. 'Your bag's at my apartment. It's just a few blocks from here, we can walk over there. And I'll send someone from Lincoln Center to pick mine up from your hotel tomorrow.'

Serena hesitated. 'Um, Joseph . . .'

'Hey, only my grandmother calls me that. I'm Joe.'

'OK, Joe. Well, you're going to think I'm being silly, but . . .'

'I get it,' he broke in. 'You're not comfortable going to a stranger's apartment. And I don't blame you. Even opera singers can be bad guys.'

'Oh, I wasn't implying—' she began, but he held up his hand.

'Really, I understand. How about this? You go back to your hotel. I'll pick up your suitcase and bring it over. Then I can get mine and I won't have to send someone tomorrow.'

'OK,' Serena said. 'I'm at the Palladium Hotel, on Madison Avenue.' She turned and started towards the street.

'Hey, wait a minute!'

She turned.

'It would help if I had your name,' he said with a

163

smile. Not just a smile – a gorgeous wide grin that lit up his face.

She flushed again. 'Of course. I'm Serena Kent.'

He nodded. 'See you later, Serena Kent.'

Serena knew she was within walking distance of the hotel, but she decided to splurge on a taxi. She was feeling oddly dazed.

Back at the hotel, she went up to her room and checked to make sure the gowns were neatly packed. She considered taking a shower but she was afraid she wouldn't hear the phone if reception called to announce Joe Feldman's arrival. So she simply brushed her teeth, ran a comb through her hair and sat down to wait.

She felt like she was waiting for a long time. Maybe he wasn't going to come, she thought. After all, he didn't desperately need his suitcase. She may have blown her chance to get her own back. Why was she such a prude? Jennifer would have gone back to the singer's apartment without a thought. Now he probably thought she was just some kind of virginal prig.

That was when she realised she didn't only want to see her suitcase again. She wanted to see *him*.

She jumped up when the phone rang.

'Hello?'

'Miss Kent, you have a visitor here at the desk. A Mr Feldman.'

'I'll be right down,' she said, and hung up. Once again, she felt so stupid. She could have told the desk to send him up to her room. Maybe she really was a virginal prig.

She carried the suitcase down to the lobby and saw Joe Feldman, holding an identical suitcase, standing by the reception desk.

'Would you like to trade?' he asked.

They exchanged suitcases.

'Thank you for bringing it here,' Serena said.

'My pleasure,' he replied.

There was a moment of silence. He really was very cute, she thought. Kind of like a teddy bear, but sexy. Huggable.

'Well . . .' he began.

He was going to leave, and she would never see him again. Suddenly, she knew she couldn't let that happen.

'Could – could I buy you a drink?' she asked impulsively. 'To thank you?'

She couldn't believe she'd just done that. Never before in her life had she been so forward with a man.

But Joe Feldman wasn't shocked. 'I'd like that.'

They left their suitcases with the receptionist at the desk, and went into the hotel bar. The pre-dinner drinks people were gone, the late-night crowd hadn't yet arrived, so they were able to get a booth.

Serena studied the long list of cocktails. Not being a drinker, they meant nothing to her. And she was a little worried about ordering alcohol anyway. The waiter might ask for ID.

'I think I'll just have juice,' she murmured.

He grinned. 'I'm not twenty-one yet either.' So they ordered cranberry juice and sparkling water, which at least looked like cocktails.

'You know, if either of us had less boring, run-of-the-mill suitcases, this wouldn't have happened,' Joe said.

'I know,' Serena said. 'It's funny, when I bought that suitcase, there was another one in the store that was hot pink. I should have taken that one.'

'Except, then we would never have met,' Joe remarked.

She smiled uncertainly, not knowing how to respond to that, and was relieved when the drinks arrived. Joe lifted his.

'Let's drink to ordinary suitcases.'

With a slightly less uncertain smile, she clinked her glass with his.

'You must be tired, if you only arrived last night,' Serena said.

'You arrived last night too,' he reminded her.

'But I didn't just finish a week-long run of the opera in London,' she said. 'A very successful run!'

'Did you see it there?'

'No, I don't live in London. But I saw the reviews. I can't tell you how thrilled I was when I learned that the opera was running here in New York.'

He smiled. 'You're a big opera fan?'

'Oh yes,' she said. 'I listen to opera music all the time. But this is the first real opera I've ever seen.' For the third time that evening, she wanted to kick herself. Now he'd think she was a total barbarian.

But he actually seemed interested. 'You're not one of those people who think it's a travesty to mess around with Mozart?'

'Not at all,' she said promptly. 'I mean, the original music is wonderful. But I think that art must evolve, and it's the obligation of artists to experiment. People take art too seriously; they treat it like it's sacred. But I believe that—' She caught herself. This was just the kind of talk that bored her friends to death.

But Joe didn't look bored. In fact, he was nodding with enthusiasm. 'Exactly! You know, I studied classical opera, and I appreciate it, but this production was a lot more fun than most of the work I've done.' He lowered his voice. 'That's just between us though, OK? I'm up for a big role in *Don Giovanni*, and I don't want anyone to think I'm not into the classics!'

She liked that 'just between us' comment. She liked the way he looked too. It was ironic, how she'd thought the owner of the gowns in the suitcase was tall. That was only because she'd assumed the owner was a woman. Joe wasn't short, but no one would call him a tall man. He wasn't exactly handsome, either, not in the classic sense. Jennifer probably wouldn't give a guy like this a second look.

But Serena liked looking at him. Very much. His eyes were warm, and they sparkled. And he had a rumpled look that she found appealing. Clearly, he wasn't the kind of person who spent hours grooming and admiring himself in the mirror, like most celebrities probably did.

'Can I ask you a personal question?' she asked boldly.

'Yeah, sure.'

'How old are you?'

'That *is* personal,' he said. 'But it's also in my bio in the programme.'

She flushed. 'I haven't had a chance to read the programme.'

'Good for you,' he said.

'Huh?'

'Only people who are bored with a performance read programmes while the show is going on. Anyway, in answer to your question, I'm nineteen.'

Even younger than she'd thought. 'So am I,' she said. 'It's so impressive, to be where you are at that age.'

'What do you do?' he asked.

'Nothing quite as impressive,' she said. 'I'm studying art history at a university at home.'

'Aha!' he exclaimed. 'That explains *Spiritual Motifs in Art of the High Renaissance*.'

'My thesis topic,' she said.

'That sounds pretty impressive to me,' he said. 'What are you doing in New York? Is this a vacation?'

'Actually, I'm just here for the weekend,' she said.

'Wow,' he remarked. 'Are you some kind of jet-setter?'

'*No*, not at all.' Would he think she was some kind of lowbrow TV addict if she told him how she came to be here? Oh, what did it matter? She was always worrying how she came across to a guy, and it never got her anywhere. She might as well be honest. So she told him the whole story of *Babes in Manhattan* and the contest, and then waited to see how deeply it would turn him off her.

But it didn't. He burst out laughing. 'I have a

169

confession to make. I've never seen *Babes in Manhattan*. But do you know "Rehab"? That terrible medical reality show? I'm totally addicted!'

Then he wasn't so artsy that he couldn't enjoy a little trashy TV. He was smart, he was good-looking, he was talented – and what was truly amazing was the fact that she was actually comfortable with him. She couldn't remember ever having such a good evening on a date. Mentally, she corrected herself. This wasn't a date, it was just an accidental meeting.

He yawned, and then he clapped his hand over his mouth. 'I'm sorry. I guess I really am wiped out.'

'That's all right,' she said kindly. She couldn't expect the evening to go on for ever. At least now she had one good memory of an encounter with a guy.

'I'll feel better tomorrow,' he said. 'And I'm not singing tomorrow night. Would you like to go out?'

It seemed to her that she was having a hard time speaking, and suddenly it was taking way too long to come up with any kind of response. Finally, one came out.

'Yes.'

As they left the bar, her head was spinning. Was it possible? Could she actually come away from this trip with *two* good memories?

Chapter Fifteen

Megan was having a very strange dream. Her hands were held behind her back with handcuffs. She was being arrested for something, but she had no idea what she had done. Strangely enough, she wasn't frightened or even apprehensive. In the dream, her situation seemed totally natural and right.

When she woke up, her hands were clasped together behind her back. Still not completely alert, she unclasped them and examined her wrists. There was no evidence of any restrictive device. But of course not, it was a crazy dream. Megan wasn't a big believer in dream interpretation, but she couldn't help wondering what it might have meant.

She glanced towards the other bed in the room. Erica was still completely unconscious, which was a good thing as far as Megan was concerned. When her roommate woke up, she would have a massive hangover, so she might as well sleep as long as possible. Thank goodness Jennifer and Nick had shown up last night at the Cottage. By the time Erica had finished her third mojito, she was staggering, and Megan had been grateful to have the others there to help get her back to the hotel.

But at least taking care of Erica had kept Megan's mind off Frank McGuire. He was popping back into her head now, so to ward off the thoughts she got out of bed and headed to the shower. She was just about to turn the water on when she heard the phone ringing. Thank goodness for the bathroom phone – she was able to grab it before the noise woke Erica.

'Ms Briggs, please.'

'Speaking.'

'This is the front desk. You have a special delivery from the National Bank of the United Kingdom here.'

'Wow! That was quick . . . Thank you, I'll be down to pick it up shortly,' Megan said. It had to be her new credit and debit cards. She'd almost forgotten about the missing wallet. This was good news – she could now continue shopping. Strange, though, that she didn't feel more cheerful.

She showered, put on the lovely thick robe provided by the hotel and went into the sitting room. Serena and

Jennifer were drinking tea at the table, and Serena was talking.

'. . . and he asked me out tonight!'

Megan perked up. 'Who? What? Tell, tell!'

She was impressed with Serena's tale of finding her suitcase, meeting an opera singer and having a drink with him at the bar.

'He sounds like a nice guy. This is excellent, Serena. I'll bet you never thought you'd have a romantic adventure in New York.'

'It's not a romantic adventure,' Serena said quickly. 'It was just a nice encounter.'

'But you're seeing him again tonight,' Jennifer pointed out. 'It could turn into something more.'

Serena suddenly seemed very interested in stirring her tea. 'I doubt it,' she murmured. 'He's really amazing. What would he see in someone like me?'

'Don't say that!' Jennifer exclaimed. 'You're an amazing person too. Of course, you'd be even more amazing with a decent haircut.'

'And something a little more interesting to wear,' Megan added.

'I do have my suitcase now,' Serena reminded her.

Megan and Jennifer exchanged looks. They'd been friends with Serena long enough to know that the contents of her suitcase wouldn't include anything really exciting to wear on a date.

Serena glanced at the closed door to Megan and Erica's room. 'Is Erica all right? Jen told me about your evening at the club.'

Megan shrugged. 'She's sleeping it off. We had quite a time getting her to bed last night, and I'm afraid she won't be feeling too perky when she wakes up, but she'll be OK.' She turned to Jennifer. 'I didn't even get a chance last night to ask you about the concert. How was it?'

'Fabulous,' Jennifer replied. 'He's even better live than on his recordings.' She sighed. 'I can't believe he's staying right here in this hotel.'

'Are you sure he's still here?' Serena asked. 'Now that the concert is over, he might have checked out.'

Jennifer shook her head. 'There's another concert tonight, so he's here. Of course, I don't have a chance in hell of hooking up with him in the hotel. Not with Nick around.'

'Actually, I don't think Nick is on duty today,' Megan remarked.

Jennifer raised her eyebrows. 'How do you know that?'

'I just had a call from the desk telling me that my new cards from the bank are here. And the person who called wasn't Nick.'

'There's more than one receptionist at the desk,' Jennifer reminded her, adding a little too casually, 'Nick was nice last night, wasn't he?'

'Very,' Megan said, hiding a knowing smile. She turned to Serena. 'What are you doing today?'

'I'm going to the Guggenheim Museum,' Serena said.

Jennifer looked up. 'Really? I might go with you.'

Megan stared at her. 'You're kidding! You want to go to a museum?'

'I'll go to *that* museum,' Jennifer said. 'Look.' She went to her handbag and took out a new magazine she'd bought the day before. Leafing through it, she stopped at a page and showed it to the others.

Serena read the photo caption aloud. ' "Reese Witherspoon checks out the contemporary art at the Guggenheim Museum." Jen, this doesn't mean she goes every day.'

'But it means celebrities do go there,' Jennifer declared. 'And I'm tired of standing around in front of expensive restaurants.'

'Do you want to come?' Serena asked Megan.

'No, now that I've got a credit card again, I'm going to shop.'

Thirty minutes later, after picking up her cards at the

desk, Megan was standing in front of the hotel and trying to decide which way to go. She'd read that you could find great bargains on the Lower East Side. And she hadn't really explored the shops in Greenwich Village yet. Or maybe she should go back to that store on Fifth Avenue and see if the orange alligator handbag was still there.

For some reason, none of these ideas got her feeling excited. Was it possible she could have burned out on shopping? No, that was inconceivable. Maybe it was the weather. The sky was grey, there was a chill in the air and she was afraid of getting caught in a downpour. There were people selling umbrellas on almost every street corner, but even so, the idea of strolling around and going from store to store in less-than-ideal weather didn't appeal to her.

Because she liked everything to be perfect. Because she was a spoiled princess.

And then suddenly she knew where it was she wanted to go. She started walking with a purpose and a clear destination in mind.

It didn't take long before she found herself in front of the police station. Inside, it looked pretty much the same as yesterday. The people probably weren't the same ones who'd been there the day before, but they were in similar states of distress, anger and hostility. Resolutely, she joined the long queue at the desk. She was determined to wait as long as she had to in order to make her enquiry.

But she was in luck – the object of her mission came out of a door. She almost missed him because he wasn't in his uniform, but the face was unmistakeable. He headed for the exit. She left the queue and went after him.

She caught up with him just outside on the steps. 'Excuse me, Officer McGuire?'

He turned, and when he saw her he held his hands up, as if to ward off a blow. 'Oh, no.'

'This will only take a minute,' she promised.

'Lady, I'm off duty,' he said.

'But I need to talk to you—'

He wouldn't let her finish. Pointing back at the building, he said, 'There's a hundred other cops in there, Miss. They'll be happy to take your statement.' He turned away and continued down the steps.

'But I want to talk to *you*!' she cried out.

He paused, and looked back at her. 'Miss Briggs—'

'You remember my name?' she said, raising an eyebrow.

'You're unforgettable,' he said.

She didn't think that was exactly a compliment, but she brushed it off. 'Call me Megan.'

He sighed. 'OK, Megan, I've just finished two shifts. I'm tired and I'm hungry and—'

She interrupted again. 'I just want to apologise.'

That kept him in place. He didn't reply, and his expression didn't tell her anything, but at least he wasn't moving. Encouraged, she continued.

'I was wrong yesterday. I shouldn't have bothered you or yelled at you. I was upset about my wallet, but that's no excuse. I know you have more important crimes to deal with and I shouldn't have been so demanding. So, I'm sorry.'

He nodded. 'OK.'

'And I didn't file a complaint about you.'

'OK,' he said again. And he turned as if to proceed down the steps.

'Wait!' Megan yelled.

He stopped again and turned. She could see the weariness on his face, but she couldn't let him go. When would she have this opportunity again?

'What?' he asked.

What else could she say to keep him listening? 'Um . . . well, you could say "thank you".'

He looked bewildered.

Megan spoke rapidly. 'I mean, I came all the way over here just to apologise to you. I only have three days here in New York, and there are a lot of other things I could be doing instead of hanging around at a police station.'

He nodded. 'Then why don't you just go ahead and do them?'

Her insides were churning, and she could feel irritation joining all the other mixed-up emotions she was feeling. The distress must have shown on her face because he finally spoke again.

'OK, I accept your apology. Thank you for offering it.'

She could have sworn she caught a twinkle in those green eyes, but it might have been her imagination. In any case, she didn't have long to look. He turned and walked down the steps.

He looked nice from behind. Nice jeans, not too tight or baggy. Nice bum. Green sweatshirt. Had he picked it to match his eyes?

She watched as he turned to the right and walked down the street. For some reason, in her mind she heard Jennifer saying how she wouldn't pass up any opportunity to connect with a celebrity. She hurried down the steps and turned to the right.

She could see him at the corner, making another right.

She followed, turned the corner and saw him walk into a café, the kind they called a 'diner' in New York. Edging closer, she looked in the window. It looked like one of those places she'd seen in movies set in New York, with red booths, shiny wood tables, a counter with stools, and an old-fashioned jukebox in the corner. Frank sat down at a booth and opened the menu that was lying there. Seconds later a waitress appeared at his side. Megan saw his lips move and the waitress jot something down on her pad and then walk away.

So he'd ordered, which meant he wouldn't walk out. And Megan walked in.

He glanced up as she approached his booth, his expression surprised, but not exactly angry when he saw her. His first words weren't very welcoming though.

'Are you stalking me?' he asked. 'That's against the law in this country, you know.'

She fumbled for words. 'Look, maybe this sounds crazy, but . . . I feel like we have some unfinished business.'

'Huh?'

'We got off on the wrong foot,' she said. 'And . . . and I think you have the wrong impression of me. I'm not the kind of person you think I am.'

'What kind of person is that?' he asked.

'A spoiled princess. That's what you called me. And maybe I am, a little. I've always got everything I wanted – without working for it.'

A flicker of a smile crossed his face. 'How nice for you.'

'But it's not my fault!' she said. 'Not completely. I couldn't help being an only child, or having parents who are well off and who dote on me. It's not my fault that I ended up being a little spoiled. OK, *very* spoiled. But that doesn't make me a bad person!'

He looked at her thoughtfully. 'All right, I won't blame you for your snotty attitude.'

She gasped and glared at him. 'I am *not* snotty!'

Now she could see a real smile. 'OK, my turn to apologise. Would you like to sit down?'

One teeny-tiny element of Megan Briggs wanted to turn away and storm out. But the rest of Megan wanted something else. She slid into the seat opposite him.

The waitress reappeared, bearing a tray of eggs, bacon and fried potatoes and placed it in front of Frank McGuire. 'What can I get you?' she asked Megan.

'Just coffee, please,' Megan said.

'Not tea?' the policeman asked. 'Didn't you say you're from England?'

'Not all English people drink tea all the time,' Megan

said. 'That's just one of the stereotypes you Americans believe about us.'

'What's another one?' he asked, looking amused.

Megan thought about it. 'There are people here who think we're all either cockneys or aristocrats. I guess that comes from the TV shows. Or the way we speak. In any case, I can tell you now that I have never met a member of the royal family, and I have never referred to the police as the "Old Bill".'

'So you're not Lady Megan Briggs?' he said, a definite twinkle in his eyes.

She shook her head. 'I'm just plain Megan.'

He reached his right hand across the table. 'How do you do, just plain Megan. I'm just plain Frank.'

She took his hand and shook it.

'So . . . what are you doing in New York?' he asked.

She told him about the TV show and the competition and her friends. 'We each came here with a particular agenda. Serena wanted to go to museums. Erica had an online friend to meet and Jennifer's looking for celebrities.'

'What about you?'

'I just wanted to shop.'

He gazed at her quizzically. 'That's it?'

'Well, I came here as a child with my parents, so I've

seen all the major sights. And the dollar is weak compared to the pound, so everything costs a lot less here. And buying things just makes me happy!'

His next question was unexpected. 'Why?'

'Why?' she repeated. 'Well, because . . . because . . . it's what I like to do.' It was a dumb answer, but she couldn't think of any other reason. It was time to change the subject.

'About my wallet,' she said. 'I'm thinking now that you could have been right. Maybe it wasn't stolen and I *did* leave it somewhere. I should probably go and retrace my steps from yesterday.'

He nodded. 'Are you sure you don't want anything to eat?'

'No, thank you.'

'Well then, if you'll wait until I finish eating, I'll retrace your steps with you.'

Someone must have put money in the jukebox, because suddenly there was music. Megan recognised the song. One of those old-time love songs. As the chorus kicked in, she heard Frank Sinatra's sultry voice.

'Ah. "It had to be you",' said Frank, taking a minute to savour the words. For a second, he locked eyes with Megan, and she saw the slight colour in his face. Though he looked away quickly, she couldn't help her heart skip a tiny beat.

She smiled and glanced out of the window. The weather hadn't changed at all. But somehow, everything looked sunnier.

Chapter Sixteen

Erica was relieved to find that they had painkillers in the hotel shop. She'd already taken two that she'd cadged from Megan earlier, but she felt very certain that she would need more very soon. Why did anyone drink mojitos if they knew they would feel like this in the morning?

She paused in front of a display of sunglasses. She'd already noted that it was grey outside, but she would have liked to cover her bloodshot eyes. Still, she'd probably look ridiculous wearing shades on a day like this. She decided not to buy any, and just hope'd that by the time of her meeting with Danny the redness in her eyes would have disappeared.

Proceeding carefully, knowing that the slightest abrupt movement could cause severe pain, she paid for the painkillers and then made her way through the lobby.

Once outside, she leaned against the building and took a deep breath of not-very-fresh New York air. She was still feeling pretty fragile, and not quite ready to merge onto the crowded sidewalk. The sound of a passing ambulance made her wince.

How much alcohol had she consumed last night? She'd never been much of a drinker. The occasional beer at a pub, a glass of wine or two if she went out to dinner – that was about all she could handle. She'd never had a mojito before last night. It was very tasty, especially with all that mint, but it was now on her list of drinks never to be consumed again.

She couldn't remember the last time she'd felt so physically wretched. Not to mention embarrassed. It was one thing to get so horribly drunk in front of mates – they'd seen each other tipsy before. But in front of a total stranger, like Nick . . . She'd been extremely grateful that he wasn't at the reception desk that morning, and she hoped he wouldn't be there for the rest of the weekend.

She knew why she'd indulged so much. She'd been trying not to think about Danny. But why had she been so upset about him? So what if he couldn't have dinner with her last night? He probably had a very good reason. He hadn't really blown her off; he wanted to see her again. Why had she reacted so strongly?

Dumb question. It was because she was falling in love with him.

The shock of this realisation hit her, hard. How could this be? She'd only met him the day before. Yes, they'd been communicating for ages online, but that wasn't the same as really knowing a person, was it? He was an interesting friend, a pleasant companion, and there was an attraction for sure, but how could she call it love?

But she had other interesting friends and pleasant companions. This was different. It didn't feel like a crush. It was something deeper, stronger; something she had never felt before. There was a connection that she couldn't explain; an indefinable and inexplicable bond that linked them. And somehow, even though he'd left her yesterday, she knew he felt it too. She didn't know *how* she knew – but she was certain of it.

But then, why wasn't he taking advantage of their situation? She was only here for three days, shouldn't he be making more effort? Or maybe this was all her own fantasy, the after-effects of her drinking binge. Did hangovers stir the imagination?

She was beginning to feel a little sturdier, and she looked at her watch. It was just after eleven and their meeting was at noon. She had plenty of time to walk, clear her head and be able to greet him as a reasonably normal person.

By the time she reached the corner of 72nd Street and Park Avenue, she *was* feeling much better. The headache was gone and the noise of the street wasn't bothering her any more.

But she still felt sick. Was she in love? She hardly knew him!

She stopped in a doorway and pulled out a compact to check her face. Her eyes were no longer red, and she didn't see any other evidence of her escapade. She swept some gloss across her lips, closed the compact and checked her watch again. She was ten minutes early. She supposed she could kill time and walk around the block, but that was when she felt a few drops of rain. She ducked under the awning of Danny's building.

An elegantly uniformed man opened the door and let her into the grand lobby of the building. Gilt-edged mirrors on the walls, oriental rugs on the floor, some richly upholstered chairs . . . yes, this was exactly the kind of building she had expected Danny to live in.

'May I help you?' the doorman asked.

'Yes, I'm here to see Danny Parsons,' she said.

His brow furrowed. 'Parsons?

'Yes, Danny Parsons?'

'There isn't anyone named Parsons living here. Could he be visiting one of our residents?'

'No, this is where he lives.' Erica rummaged in her bag for her diary. 'Oh, wait, maybe I have the wrong street number.'

But the address she had written in her diary was the address of this building. She was about to point this out to the doorman when he turned away to let another person into the building. A flustered-looking Danny entered.

'May I help—' the doorman began but Danny ignored him and turned, smiling, to Erica.

'Am I late or are you early?' Not waiting for her to respond, he took her arm. 'Let's go.'

He hurried her out, putting up a large umbrella to cover them both from the light rain.

'I thought I had the wrong building,' Erica told him. 'The doorman said there was no one called Parsons there.'

Danny shook his head wearily. 'That guy's new, and really pompous. He hasn't learned all the tenants's names yet but he's too proud to admit it.'

'I was rather hoping I could see your flat,' Erica told him. And then she remembered what one of the girls had said the day before. Maybe he *was* married. Maybe, right this minute, Mrs Danny Parsons was up there running a vacuum cleaner over their carpet.

'No way!' Danny said with a look of mock terror. 'It's a total mess. I'm a complete slob, and the cleaning lady's on vacation. When she's away, my apartment looks like the aftermath of a hurricane.' He looked at her with an expression of exaggerated concern. 'Uh-oh. I hope you're not some kind of manic neat-freak.'

'Hardly,' she said, somewhat mollified by his response, 'and unfortunately, I don't have a cleaning lady, so my room pretty much stays a mess all the time. Oh look, it's stopped raining.'

'Good,' Danny said. 'Because this would be hard to do with one hand.' He closed the umbrella, dropped it by his side and took Erica in his arms. And even though it was a total surprise to her, she found herself falling easily and snugly into the embrace.

The kiss seemed to go on for ever, and that was fine by her. She didn't know if passers-by were staring at them, and she didn't care. It all felt so right, natural and effortless, like something they were meant to do. And when they finally stopped kissing, there was no embarrassment, no discomfort, no awkwardness at all. They just stared at each other with an understanding and acceptance of what had just happened. And she knew she'd been right – he felt the same connection.

They walked along the street for a while, hand in hand, comfortable in the silence. Danny spoke first.

'What would you like to do today?'

She gave him a sideways glance and what she hoped was a sexy smile. He grinned.

'Hey, I told you, my place is off-limits. Maybe I should have asked, what would you like to *see* today?'

You, she thought. Just you. But aloud, she said, 'I don't know. The sun's coming out, we could do something outdoors. Walk around Central Park?'

'There are other outdoor places in New York,' he told her. 'I've got an idea. I know you're supposed to be a babe in Manhattan, but are you willing to explore another borough?'

They descended the stairs into the noisy, crowded subway station. She didn't see the dirt this time, and the harsh sounds didn't bother her at all. She was still floating on the memory of that kiss. She wanted to make more memories, right here and now, but the train came along and they were swept into the standing-room-only carriage. They could barely keep their hands clasped, let alone speak or do anything else. So she closed her eyes, and simply allowed herself to enjoy the unbelievable happiness she was feeling. All the insecurities, the worries of the day before had vanished. Even her shame about last night's behaviour was gone. None of that mattered any more.

The train stopped and the doors opened. 'Welcome to Brooklyn,' Danny said, and keeping a firm grip on her hand, he got them both out of the carriage.

The neighbourhood they emerged into had a completely different look to Manhattan. The brownstone houses had a warm, relaxed feel to them, and there were lots of kids on skateboards or Rollerblades, and parents pushing prams.

'Most of these brownstones are from the Victorian period,' Danny told her. 'It was a very grand area at that time, and then it went downhill and became almost a slum. Then it went through gentrification and now it's one of the most desirable places to live in New York.'

At the top of the street, across the road, was a huge park that stretched as far as she could see. 'That's Prospect Park,' Danny continued. 'It was built in the 1860s, and designed by the same guys who made Central Park.'

'You know a lot about New York,' Erica commented.

'I love this city, Erica.' His eyes were soft and his voice was low. 'It's the most exciting place on earth. Every opportunity you could imagine in life, the possibilities . . .

they're all here. You can become anyone you want in New York. You can create your own future. This is the city of the self-made man.'

'And woman?' Erica asked.

He smiled. 'Absolutely. If you have the guts and the determination to succeed, you can do it here, easier than any other place on earth. I'm not saying we don't have the rich/poor divide – and some people are definitely born into privilege but there's no rigid class system. Nobody really cares who your family is, where you came from. You can succeed on your own.'

'Like you did,' Erica said.

The smile seemed to fade slightly, but then it returned, wider than before. 'Right. Come on, let's go.'

'Where?'

He led her around the side of the park, past an oval plaza with a huge arch where some sort of market seemed to be going on, then past a library and finally stopped at an entrance to the Brooklyn Botanic Gardens. Inside, they wandered along winding paths. At this time of year, there weren't many flowers in bloom, but the foliage on the trees made up for it with a spectacle of gold, red, orange and yellow. They walked across a wooden bridge over a pond and explored the serene beauty of the Japanese Garden. There were other people walking around the garden too, but it wasn't crowded.

Danny clearly knew the place well. He pointed out the cherry trees and told her about the spring festival that was held here when the trees blossomed. He showed her the rose garden and described the summer blooms so well she could practically see the flowers. They explored the Shakespeare Garden, where plants mentioned in Shakespeare's plays and poems were displayed.

And by a lovely waterfall, right there in the Botanic Garden, he took her in his arms and kissed her again.

It was while they were still in each other's arms that she heard his stomach growl.

'You're hungry,' she declared. 'And so am I.'

'It's two-thirty,' he pointed out. 'We forgot about lunch. Want to grab a hot dog in the park?'

When she hesitated, he added, 'Or if you're not in the mood for a hot dog, we could stop in a coffee shop?'

'It's not that,' she said. 'One of the reasons I wanted to go to your flat is because I thought I might cook us a meal.'

'Oh.' He looked uncomfortable. 'I don't think there's anything to cook at my place. I go out to eat a lot, you know. And by the time we bought stuff and got back there . . .'

'It's OK,' she assured him. 'Maybe tomorrow.'

'You're leaving tomorrow,' he reminded her.

It was as if she'd completely blanked out the fact. Hearing him say it made her feel almost physically ill.

'I have an idea,' he said suddenly. 'I've got this . . . this cousin, who lives around here. It's just a basement studio apartment, kind of a dump, but I have his keys. Because he's out of town and I've been picking up his mail.'

She brightened. 'We could buy some ingredients at that market we passed and I could make lunch there.'

He nodded. 'Let's do it.'

They strolled through the market, and Erica looked for inspiration. She found it in a stack of ripe orange pumpkins.

'I'm going to make you pumpkin soup,' she declared. 'I've been playing around with a recipe and I think I'm ready to show it off.' She located everything she needed for the soup – fresh ginger, sticks of cinnamon, onions and garlic. They gathered some gorgeous greens for a salad, and a freshly baked loaf of brown bread, and headed back to the brownstone neighbourhood where Danny's cousin had his flat.

It was located in one of the pretty Victorian houses, but they didn't go up the steps to the main entrance. Danny led her down some side steps to a door, and they went in.

Erica wouldn't have called it a dump exactly. It was reasonably clean, at least. But it was an unloved place, that was for sure. There was hardly any furniture – just a beat-up armchair and a rickety table with two folding chairs. In a corner alcove, a futon mattress lay on the floor. The walls were devoid of pictures or photos. Erica didn't care. She was alone with the man she loved, and she was going to cook for him.

As she puttered around in the tiny kitchenette, searching for appropriate pots and pans, she bemoaned the lack of good cooking utensils.

'What does your cousin do?'

'He goes to college.'

'How old is he?'

'Around my age.'

She finally found a decent carving knife and got to work on the pumpkin. 'It must be hard for him, having a cousin like you who's so successful at the same age. Is he very jealous?'

'I don't know. Hey, let's not talk about him, he's boring. Tell me about this soup you're making.'

'It's delicious, a little spicy, and perfect for this time of year. I've been experimenting with three recipes, changing ingredients and trying to make it original.'

'Have you made it in your uncle's restaurant?'

'No. He won't let me add anything new to the menu.' She sighed. 'I want to be a chef, Danny. I want to create new and exciting dishes. But I'll never get the opportunity there.'

'Have you thought about changing jobs?' he asked. 'Finding a different restaurant to work in?'

'Oh, I couldn't leave, it would upset my uncle.' She put the knife down. 'No, that's not true. He'd find someone else to chop his onions. I just don't think I could find another job. Good restaurants, they want people with certificates, qualifications, some kind of training.'

'Diplomas and degrees,' Danny said, and he sounded almost bitter. 'Yeah, I know what you mean. It's so stupid, like a piece of paper can make you good at what you do.' After a moment, he said, 'I hated school. Boring teachers forcing you to read books you didn't want to read, telling you stuff you don't want to know.'

'I wasn't much of a scholar myself,' Erica admitted. 'Although I suppose that if you're studying something you really care about, it's different.'

Danny didn't reply. When she turned to glance at him, she thought he looked grim. 'Hey, what's wrong?'

'Nothing,' he said quickly. 'I was just thinking, I could be helping you out. I'm no chef, but I think I've got the skills to wash a lettuce.'

They worked together, side by side, and talked about nothing and everything. Erica demonstrated the creation of a perfect vinaigrette – the correct proportions of oil and vinegar plus some hot Dijon mustard. Danny found an old copy of the *Wall Street Journal* and explained how to read the stock market listings. Or at least, tried to explain – it made no sense at all to Erica. And Danny was completely useless at whisking the vinaigrette properly.

The salad was ready. Danny set the table with two mismatched plates and plastic cutlery. Erica put the bread on the table, and Danny located a candle, which he lit and placed in the centre.

Erica checked the soup. 'It needs to simmer for a while,' she said. 'Thirty minutes, at least.'

'We can wait,' Danny said. And as if they'd read each other minds, they moved out of the kitchenette and towards the futon. It wasn't the most comfortable mattress Erica had ever known, but it might as well have been a four-poster bed and Danny's cousin's dreary little flat the honeymoon suite at the Ritz, for it was on this lumpy, flat futon that Erica heard words she'd only ever dreamed of hearing.

'This is going to sound crazy,' he said, 'because we

barely know each other. But I think I'm falling for you.'

She knew it was too soon. And she still had doubts. But she couldn't help herself, and without any effort, she found herself nestling into his arms, wanting to, but no quite ready to say it back.

Later, still on the futon, Erica sat up and looked around. 'Your cousin is lonely,' she said.

'How do you know that?'

'From this place. If he had a girlfriend, someone he really cared about, he'd fix it up, make it nicer for them.'

'You could be right,' Danny said looking a bit sheepish. He sniffed. 'I smell something good.'

'The soup should be just about ready,' Erica announced. She got up and glanced at her watch. 'Wow, it's already four o'clock and we're just having lunch. We won't be hungry at dinnertime.'

He got up and followed her into the kitchen. 'Erica . . .'

She began to ladle the soup into bowls. 'Hmm?'

'I can't have dinner with you tonight.'

Her hand wavered, and a little drop of soup dripped down the side of a bowl. 'No?'

'I'm so sorry, I'd give anything to spend every minute of this weekend with you. But I've got another work thing.'

'On Saturday night?'

'I know, it's bizarre, but . . . but that's how it is. Clients, you know. I have to see them. And if there was any way I could get out of it, I would. But I can't.'

She set the bowls on the table. 'That's all right.'

'Really?' he asked. 'Is it really all right? Because what I said before . . . I meant it, Erica. I've never felt like this about anyone before in my life.' He put his hands on her shoulders and turned her to face him. 'Do you believe me?' His voice cracked. 'I have to know that you believe me!'

His eyes were filled with tears. But beyond the tears, the light of honesty and love shone through.

'I believe you,' she whispered. And then, before her own tears could appear, she said, 'Now sit down and eat before the soup gets cold.'

Chapter Seventeen

Jennifer loved the bathroom that was connected to the room she shared with Serena. And what she loved most about it was the mirror.

It was enormous, covering a large section of a wall. Thanks to the hotel's housekeeping service, it was always clean and shiny. And best of all, it was surrounded by tiny lights that made it impossible to miss anything. Like those slightly darkened areas under her eyes, the result of yesterday's late night. Deftly, she applied some concealing cream.

She stepped back and took in her whole look. She'd copied it from that photo of Reese Witherspoon at this museum, the Google-something. Slim dark jeans, a white shirt, a bright red and blue scarf around her neck. Hair pulled back or left loose? She tried both, and decided that pulled back gave her a more artsy look. Objectively speaking, she knew she looked fabulous.

She came out of the bathroom and Serena looked up from where she was sitting on her bed, leafing through the gigantic book of paintings she'd dragged along to New York.

'Ready?'

Jennifer nodded. 'Your turn.'

'I'm ready,' Serena said, getting up.

Jennifer groaned. 'Honestly, Serena, you *cannot* wear that again today. It's all wrinkled!'

Serena looked down at the brown skirt. 'Is it?'

'You've got your suitcase back, you must have something else to put on. Now change your clothes and meet me in the lobby.' With that, Jennifer picked up her bag and left the suite.

Down in the lobby, she sauntered over to the reception desk. A young woman looked up and smiled professionally.

'Yes, may I help you?'

'Is Nick on duty today?' she asked.

The receptionist's eyebrows went up. '*Mr Caine* is not here at the moment.'

Jennifer ignored the way the woman had said the name. 'Will he be coming in later today?'

The professional smile had become a bit frosty. 'I

really can't say, Miss, I don't have the schedule at hand. May *I* assist you in some way?'

'No,' Jennifer said, and started to turn away. Then she looked back. 'Is Jordan Blake still in his room? And don't tell me he's not staying here, I've seen him.'

Now the woman's smile was icy. 'I'm very sorry, but we do not divulge information about our guests.'

'Yes, yes, I know,' Jennifer said, and walked away. There was no point searching the lobby or the bar for him. Jordan Blake was probably still sleeping. She wondered where he'd partied last night. When she heard the lift doors open, she couldn't help looking up, but it was only Serena.

She didn't look much better than she'd looked in the hotel room. Shapeless jeans with a baggy, faded red jumper. Sometimes it was hard loving a friend who was so hopeless.

It was raining so they splurged on a taxi uptown. Serena jabbered about the paintings they were going to see, while Jennifer spent most of the time worrying that her hair would frizz in this weather.

'There it is,' Serena squealed excitedly. 'Isn't it amazing?'

It was certainly the strangest looking building Jennifer had ever seen. It was round and white, and in her opinion it resembled a wedding cake.

'It was designed by Frank Lloyd Wright, and it's considered to be one of the most important works of architecture in the world,' Serena said.

'Certainly one of the weirdest,' Jennifer commented. Inside, it was even stranger. Instead of stairs leading from one level to the next, the floor spiralled up like a gigantic ramp. Perfect for Rollerblading, she thought. She envisioned herself cruising around the curves.

An hour later, she was still thinking about that. As far as she was concerned, Rollerblading through the Guggenheim Museum would be a lot more fun than looking at the pictures and listening to Serena's earnest observations on each one. At that moment, she was going on and on about a canvas covered with lines and a few splashes of colour.

'You can see how Picasso deals with the artist's perception of himself here. Notice how through the use of schematic forms he removes the figure of the artist from the world of ordinary people.'

'Serena, I don't notice anything at all,' Jennifer said impatiently, 'and I'm getting bored.'

'But there's still so much to see,' Serena protested.

'And more important things to do,' Jennifer countered. 'Serena, you've got a date tonight, right?'

'I don't know that I'd call it a date,' Serena demurred.

'A man has invited you to have dinner with him. I think I can safely inform you, my dear clueless friend, that this is a date.'

Serena shrugged. 'OK, it's a date. What about it?'

'Well, do you like him?' Jennifer demanded.

Serena reddened. 'I . . . I don't really know him. But he seems very nice, and we're into a lot of the same things, and I think . . .'

'You like him,' Jennifer stated.

Serena grinned. 'I think I could.'

'Then you need some help before you see him tonight,' Jennifer declared firmly.

'Help with what?'

'With the way you look! Serena, I know we tease you about the way you dress and all that, and we don't care because we love you just the way you are. But men are different! They're more shallow, they're not interested in inner beauty, they want a woman to look good.'

Serena's smile disappeared. 'You think I look that bad?'

She had to be brutally honest. 'Hon, you don't look *bad*. But you could look so much better. For – what's his name?'

'Joe. He seemed to like me OK last night, the way I am.'

'Because, like you said, you have things in common. So now you can be friends, hallelujah. But if you want more, Serena, you have to work on your appearance.'

Serena didn't say anything, and Jennifer took advantage of the silence to push her case. 'You need help, Serena. Let me help you.'

Serena still wasn't smiling.

'*Please.*'

Finally, Serena sighed. 'Well, you let me drag you into a museum. I guess I could let you drag me into a shop. But don't forget, I haven't got a lot of money,' she cautioned Jen as they left the museum.

'Not to worry,' Jennifer said. 'New York is a great city for bargains. And I've got a list of designer outlet stores.'

By the time they hit the third store on her list, it was Serena's turn to complain. 'Now *I'm* bored, Jennifer. I've tried on a gazillion dresses, and you didn't like any of them.' She sat down on the little gilded chair in the dressing room, folded her arms across her chest and glared at Jennifer with an obstinate face.

Jennifer couldn't blame her for being impatient; she *had* tried on a lot of clothes. And she didn't understand the problem. Serena had an acceptable figure and most of the dresses she'd put on had fit her decently. But nothing seemed *right*. In this shop, for example, Jennifer

206

had found some really lovely things, reasonably priced, and appropriate for a dinner in New York. But not one of them seemed to do anything for Serena.

'Just one more,' Jennifer urged. She handed Serena a geometric print wrap dress with a plunging neckline. Reluctantly but obediently, Serena put it on and examined herself in the mirror.

'I can't wear this,' she declared.

'Why not?'

'It's too low, my bra shows!'

'We'll get you a new bra,' Jennifer said.

'And it's too short,' Serena continued.

'Rubbish, it's longer than any dress I own,' Jennifer stated. 'Of course, it's terrible with those shoes. We wear the same size, I'll lend you a pair of mine. And a purse too.'

Serena didn't look convinced. 'I don't know, Jennifer. Do you really think this suits me?'

Actually, Jennifer couldn't say it was a spectacular look for Serena. But now, she realised why none of the clothes had been great. The body might be fine, but the rest of her wasn't. It was her hair and make-up that didn't work.

'You're buying this dress,' Jennifer decided. 'Then we'll start working on everything else.'

'What's everything else?' Serena asked.

She resisted Jennifer's effort to drag her into a hair salon. 'I just had my hair trimmed last week!'

'At some bargain cheapo chain salon,' Jennifer said disdainfully. 'And they didn't do a very good job.'

But Serena was stubborn. 'I'm not changing my hairstyle.'

Jennifer rolled her eyes. 'You don't have a style to change. Come on.' She practically dragged Serena into the salon. Unfortunately, the place was completely booked. They had to hit two more salons before they found a place where a cancellation had left a hairdresser available. Serena was still arguing with Jennifer about the necessity of this, but once the hairdresser had her robed and seated, she was too polite to continue with her protests.

'Maybe a little trim,' she began, but Jennifer took over. The hairdresser clearly saw who was in charge, and listened to Jennifer's instructions carefully. When they began talking colour, Serena forgot about courtesy and actually raised her voice.

'No! I don't want my hair coloured!'

'Hush,' Jennifer said. 'We're not talking any radical change here, Serena, just a brightening and maybe a few light streaks around the face.' She crouched down by

Serena's chair and spoke softly.

'Hon, I could be out doing something for myself right now, you know. But you're my dear friend, and I'm devoting the day to you. Because I care about you and I want you to be happy.'

Jennifer wasn't the sentimental type, and normally she wouldn't talk to her mates like this. So she knew Serena would be touched by her words. And she was right. Serena sighed and settled back in the chair. The hairdresser got to work.

An hour later, Jennifer and the hairdresser admired the results. The mousy brown hair was now a rich chestnut colour, and pale blonde streaks framed Serena's face.

'I look . . . different,' Serena said.

'Which is a good thing,' Jennifer responded practically. 'Now, on to make-up.'

'Jennifer, I'm completely broke,' Serena whispered after paying the hairdresser. 'I can't afford cosmetics.'

Jennifer considered this and came up with a solution. 'We'll go to the make-up counter of a department store and tell the salesperson you want a new look. She'll give you a whole makeover, and then you just say you're not sure about it and walk out without buying anything. If you're very careful, the make-up will last till you go out tonight.'

Serena was aghast. 'Jennifer, that's like stealing, isn't it?'

'Don't be ridiculous, I do it all the time.' She didn't add that because of this, she was well known and disliked at every cosmetic counter back home. Luckily, Serena would never have to face the irritated sales assistant here again.

But on the walk back to the hotel, Serena was still smarting from the sales assistant's annoyance. 'She looked at me like I'm a thief!'

Jennifer brushed it off with a shrug. 'Who cares? Think about how good you look.'

'You really think I look good?' Serena asked. She took a small mirror out of her bag, and examined her reflection anxiously. 'I'm afraid the black gunk on my eyes is going to smear.'

'Then you'll repair it with my stuff,' Jennifer told her with a sigh.

Serena put her mirror away and glanced at her reflection in a window. 'I just don't *feel* right.'

'It's because you don't know how to act. Now, we have to work on your personality.'

That was where Serena drew the line. 'There's nothing wrong with my personality!'

'No, of course not, but if you want to attract this

guy, you've got to flirt. What do you know about flirting, Serena?'

'Nothing,' she admitted. 'But that's because I don't believe in it. People should be natural with each other.'

'Oh, Serena, don't be ridiculous,' Jennifer said. 'You have to work at developing a relationship. I'll teach you my tricks.'

Serena shook her head. 'I don't need any tricks.'

Jennifer stopped and glared at her. 'Every woman needs tricks. Serena, who has had more success with men? You or me?' She didn't need to wait for an answer. 'Now, first off, don't talk about yourself. Even if he asks you questions, give him as little information as possible. You want to appear mysterious . . . enigmatic.'

'Why?' Serena asked.

'So he'll want to find out more about you. Conversation is like sex. You don't want to offer up too much too fast. And don't talk about what you know, art and all that. You don't want him thinking you're more intelligent than he is.'

'Well, I don't want to act stupid,' Serena said.

'Fine. Just don't act too intellectual. If he's talking about something you know about, make your eyes go wide and act impressed, like you're hearing it for the first time. And do a subtle sexy look from time to time.'

'What's a subtle sexy look?'

'Watch me.' Jennifer ducked her head, tilted it sideways, and with her face down, she looked to her right, at Serena, without turning her head in that direction. And smiled, just slightly.

Serena was impressed. 'That *is* sexy.'

'In a subtle way,' Jennifer added. 'I got it from watching old clips of Princess Diana. She used to do it all the time. It's simple. Duck your head, tilt it to the side, look down, slide your eyes towards him, add a little smile.'

'It's complicated,' Serena said. 'I'll never remember that.'

'Just think, duck, tilt, down, slide, smile. Say it.'

Serena repeated, 'Duck, tilt, down, slide, smile.'

'See, it's easy!'

'Easy to say,' Serena murmured. 'Not so easy to do.'

There was more – a lot more. Serena felt like she should be taking notes the way she did in her classes. By the time they arrived at the hotel, Jennifer had given Serena a complete crash course on how to attract and interest a man. Jennifer was pleased with herself. She was confident that, with a little practice, Serena just might have a hope of making something happen with her opera guy.

'Go on up to the room and find my black stilettos,

212

they'll be perfect with the new dress,' she instructed her student. 'I'll be up shortly and we can work on your moves.'

'Right,' Serena said reluctantly. 'Where are you going?'

'I want to see if Nick is working at the desk.'

'Why?'

'Just to say hello. And don't forget to practise walking in my black stilettos.'

Serena headed to the lift, while Jennifer made her way to the front desk. She didn't see Nick, and the other receptionists were busy, so she waited. Then she noticed a huge bouquet of plastic-wrapped flowers lying on the counter. They looked just like the ones Erica had received when they arrived, and she wondered if the online boyfriend had sent her more. She moved close enough to read the name on the little envelope that dangled from the bouquet.

They were for Jordan Blake. Jennifer gazed at them for a moment, and debated. Maybe it was a good thing that Nick wasn't around. Quickly checking to make sure no one from behind the desk was watching, she picked up the bouquet, and walked rapidly to the lift.

Pressing the button for the penthouse floor, she considered the possibilities. If that same man, the agent or manager or whoever he was, opened the door, she'd just thrust the flowers at him and take off. Even if he called the desk and complained about her, how much trouble would she be in? She was just doing a favour. And there was always the possibility that the odious little man wouldn't be there.

Taking a deep breath, Jennifer rapped sharply on the door. After a few seconds, she heard a voice too muffled by the door to identify.

'Yeah?'

'Delivery,' she said loudly. 'Flowers.'

The door opened a crack. And even though she could only see part of the figure, she knew she'd lucked out. Because there he was, in all his radiant glory. Jordan Blake.

He reached out and took the flowers.

'Thanks,' he said. Then he fumbled in his pocket. Jennifer realised he was looking for some change to offer as a tip.

'Oh, I don't work here,' she said quickly. 'I just saw the flowers downstairs, and I decided to bring them up to you.' She gave him one of her sexiest smiles.

Jordan Blake looked at her suspiciously. 'Why?'

'I just wanted to tell you how much I enjoyed your concert.' Jennifer cocked her head to the side, letting her hair swing seductively.

'Yeah?' Jordan's expression turned from suspicious to interested.

Jennifer nodded, making sure to duck her head and give him her best Princess Diana sideways look.

He grinned back appreciatively. 'What's your name?' he asked.

'Jennifer.'

He studied her for a minute. Then he opened the door wider.

'Want to hang out?'

Chapter Eighteen

The bag was still there. As she entered the luxury boutique on Madison Avenue, Megan's eyes went automatically to the spot where it had been displayed the day before. There it stood, the Queen of Handbags, in all its burned orange alligator splendour. But Megan's eyes didn't linger on the magnificent item. She kept right on walking, past the handbag and to the counter where purchases were rung up.

She spotted the saleswoman who had assisted her the day before.

'Excuse me.'

The woman didn't recognise her. 'Yes, may I help you?'

Megan went into the spiel she'd already recited four times that day. 'Hello, I was here yesterday, and I've lost my wallet. I was wondering if it might have been found here.'

'I'll check.' The woman picked up a phone and pressed some numbers. 'Lost and Found? Were any wallets turned in yesterday?' She turned to Megan. 'Can you describe it?'

'Cream, long, gold-coloured metal clasp.'

The woman repeated the description, listened and said, 'Thank you.' Then she rearranged her features to appear sympathetic. 'I'm very sorry.'

Megan nodded. 'Thanks for your help.' It was too bad, this was the fifth and last store she'd visited yesterday, but she wasn't terribly upset. She had other things on her mind now. She was only sorry there weren't any more stores to check, because now she'd lose her companion.

Frank was waiting for her outside. 'Any luck?' he asked.

She shook her head. 'And that's the last store.'

Frank's sympathetic expression actually seemed sincere. 'I don't think you'll be seeing it again.'

Megan shrugged. 'Oh well, it's not the end of the world.'

'You've certainly changed your tune,' Frank remarked.

She smiled. 'I think maybe I might have overreacted yesterday. But, thank you for coming along with me. I appreciate it.'

'No problem.' he smiled. 'Sorry I couldn't go into the shops with you. But this is my beat, and even though I'm not in uniform, people might recognise me.'

'Afraid they might ask you to find a lost wallet?' Megan asked with a grin.

'No. Afraid they might panic and think there's a crime happening.'

'Oh, I understand,' she assured him. 'They're probably expecting gunfire.'

'You watch too many American crime shows,' he chided her.

She laughed. 'Probably. Those programmes make it look like bullets are flying over New York on a regular basis.' Not wanting him to think she was an aficionado of violence, she quickly added, 'Not on my favourite programme, of course.'

'Let me guess . . . *Babes in Manhattan*?' he said.

'That's right.'

'Of course,' he continued, 'a show like that carries its own stereotypes of New York. That all of us single people live like millionaires.'

So he *was* single! She'd suspected this from the way he was acting. Still, she was glad to have it confirmed. More than glad.

'Are you going to be OK without your wallet?' he asked.

She nodded. 'Thank goodness my passport wasn't in it. And the bank has already sent me replacement credit cards.'

'So now you can go right back to your mission,' he said. 'Shop till you drop.'

She spoke carefully, hoping he might take a hint. 'Actually . . . I don't feel like shopping today.'

'No? What are you going to do? You told me you've already seen all the sights.'

What to say, what to say . . . she debated the possibilities. Would it impress him if she said she wanted to visit museums? Art galleries?

'Ever been to the zoo?' he asked.

'The zoo?' she repeated stupidly.

'The Bronx Zoo,' he said. 'Biggest zoo in the USA.'

Had her parents taken her to the zoo when they came here all those years ago? She had no memory of it. Probably not. Her mother had no interest in that sort of thing. As for Megan . . . she wasn't much of an animal person either. But she decided to phrase it in a kinder way.

'I hate seeing animals in cages,' she said.

'That's what I like about *this* zoo,' he told her. 'They're free – we're the ones behind the fences. I grew up in the Bronx, and I used to go there all the time when I was a kid. Want to see it?'

Megan realised she wanted very much to know more about him, where he came from, what he was interested in. Even if it meant hanging around smelly gorilla houses.

'Sure!'

They caught a bus right there on Madison Avenue and found seats together. Sitting close by him like this, with presumably a long ride ahead of them, she felt she now had the perfect opportunity to begin her inquisition.

'You grew up in the Bronx. With two parents?'

'Yep.'

'Brothers and sisters?'

'Two older sisters.' There was a pause before he added, 'And a younger brother.'

Aha, Megan thought, noting the way the brother was mentioned as an afterthought. Sibling rivalry. Having never experienced it, that was something she'd always been curious about. 'Why did you decide to become a police officer?'

'Long story. Hey, wait a minute, you don't get to ask all the questions. It's my turn.'

Before he could ask, Megan said, 'Leicester, in an area called the Midlands. Two parents, only child. Okay, my turn.'

'Huh-uh,' he said with a grin. 'You already told me that this morning, and I haven't even been able to ask a question. Why did you decide to become – what do you do, anyway?'

'Well . . .' How was she going to make this sound good? 'My mother has a shop. Fancy knick-knacks, pottery – stuff for the home from exotic places. I work there.'

'Is it interesting? Do you like doing that?'

Suddenly, she stopped trying to embellish. For some reason, she didn't want to lie to him, not even to exaggerate.

'Actually . . . I haven't started yet. And I'm not really all that interested in Italian pots or Persian doormats. That's my mother's passion.'

'But she needs you to help her out.'

'Not really,' she admitted. 'She could easily hire someone who cares about things like that. She's doing me a favour. I need the money.' Was it necessary to add that she didn't need it for rent or food? That it would mainly subsidise her shoe collection?

'Then why not work at something you're interested in?' Frank wanted to know.

Good question. And it demanded an honest response. 'Because . . . because I don't know what I'm interested in.

I've never had a real ambition. Not like some of my mates. Serena loves art, and she's studying to work in a gallery or museum. Erica has always wanted to be a chef. Me . . . I've never had a passion.'

'Not even for shopping?' he said.

She eyed him suspiciously, but he looked serious. She grinned.

'I don't think anyone's going to pay me to do that.'

He shrugged. 'I don't know. One of my sisters, she works in the fashion industry. And isn't there such a thing called a "personal shopper"? Someone who helps other people pick out clothes?'

'That's true,' Megan said, thinking. How do you know about that?'

He grinned. 'I arrested one once for shoplifting.'

She punched him lightly on the shoulder. 'No, I don't think I want to venture into a life of crime, thank you very much.'

'There's got to be something you'd rather do than work in a shop you don't care about,' he said. 'If you have to make a living, you need to find something you enjoy, something that has meaning for you.'

She was silent for a minute. 'I guess I just haven't found it yet.' She didn't add that she hadn't even begun looking. And she didn't want this line of questioning to continue, it was making her uncomfortable.

'Okay, it's my turn,' she declared. 'Why did you want to become a cop?'

But instead of answering, he reached up and pressed the bell for the next stop. 'Let's get off here.'

Stepping off the bus, Megan saw that they were in an area that was distinctly different from everything she'd seen so far in New York. They were on a street with shops and people, but it was nothing like Madison Avenue. The shops were sad-looking businesses with shabby exteriors. Some were boarded up. Others had formidable bars over the windows. And the people weren't the chic, busy shoppers she'd been surrounded by in Manhattan. On a bench, a couple of dishevelled men passed a bottle back and forth. A weary-looking woman pushed a buggy while two small children clung to her side. A pack of teenage girls, wearing clothes that revealed more than they covered, huddled in a doorway and smoked cigarettes. A couple of young men, their faces practically hidden under the hoods of their sweatshirts, wandered aimlessly along the street.

'This is the South Bronx,' Frank said. 'Where I grew up.'

Megan looked around uneasily. 'Are we near the zoo?'

He gave a short laugh. 'Some people would say *this* is the zoo.'

She shivered, and not from the cold. It all seemed so grim. 'Why did your parents want to live here?'

'It wasn't always like this,' he told her. 'Not when they were young. It was a decent neighbourhood with hard-working people. But it changed, I don't know how. Drug dealers moved in and got a foothold here. Gangs got stronger. Businesses died, and unemployment went up. My parents didn't want to move away, they were committed to staying and working on getting the neighbourhood back in shape. Then my brother—' he stopped.

'Go on,' Megan urged.

Frank's face changed. It took on that hard expression he'd worn when he'd been so annoyed with her the day before, when he'd called her a princess. 'I don't know why I'm telling you this. You probably wouldn't understand.'

Megan faced him squarely. 'Because I grew up in a privileged world? Because I've been sheltered and coddled and protected from anything ugly? Well, maybe I don't understand. But that doesn't mean I don't care.' She wanted to say more, and she struggled to find the right words. But a sudden scream interrupted her thoughts.

She turned, and just across the street she saw a hooded figure pulling a handbag off the arm of an elderly woman. Then she saw him take something out of his pocket, and passers-by started yelling.

'Frank, look!' she cried out.

But Frank wasn't there. He was already on the other side of the street. And he was holding a gun.

It was just like on those TV shows. People ducked and ran. Megan froze. Any second now, bullets could start flying, but she was unable to move. And she wasn't even thinking about herself. What did the thief have in his hand? Could Frank get hurt?

She watched as Frank tackled the man, forcing him to drop whatever he had in his hand. Then he was talking on his mobile. Within seconds, a police car careened from around the corner, and two uniformed officers jumped out. The thief was handcuffed by one officer, the other went to help the elderly woman.

After conferring with his colleagues, Frank left the scene and returned to Megan. His expression was unreadable.

'Sorry about that,' he said abruptly. 'I shouldn't have brought you here. We'll get a bus and go on to the zoo.'

'I don't want to go to the zoo now,' Megan said. 'I want to talk about what just happened.'

'It was nothing,' he said. 'An idiot with a dinner knife that couldn't cut butter. Nobody was hurt, the lady will get her bag back. No big deal.'

'Then why do you look so upset?' she asked.

Frank pressed his lips together tightly, as if he was trying very hard to keep the words back. But she didn't look away, or change the subject. She gazed at him steadily, and willed him to share his thoughts with her.

Her will must have been pretty strong, because finally he opened his mouth and the words burst forth. 'You know how old that mugger was? He was a kid, he couldn't have been more than thirteen, fourteen. They start early around here. And who can blame them? This is what they see. This is what they learn to do.'

'What about their parents? Can't they control their children? Don't they teach them right from wrong?'

'They can have the best, most well-intentioned parents in the world, and it might not make any difference at all. They see their parents struggling, trying to make a living, pay the rent and put food on the table. Then they see the criminals, the pimps, the dealers, driving in fancy cars and throwing money around. One buddy gets involved, then another, and peer pressure rears its head.' He closed his eyes wearily.

'What will happen to that kid?' Megan asked.

Frank shrugged. 'Oh, he'll get processed as a juvenile and assigned a public defender. Some district attorney will cut a deal with the defence to avoid a trial. He'll be shipped off to a detention centre for a few months, where he'll meet more kids like himself and he'll learn more about what he can do to become a fully-fledged bad guy. Then he'll be back on the streets.'

'But surely something can be done?' Megan said. 'There has to be a way to teach these kids, to help them change . . .'

'Oh sure, people try,' Frank said. 'Parents, teachers, social workers. Religious leaders. Even cops. Everyone's looking for a way to break the cycle. Everyone's trying to talk to these kids.' His voice became bitter. 'But nobody's listening to them. We don't understand these kids, we don't really know why they become hoodlums.'

Megan shuddered. 'You make it sound hopeless.'

Frank managed a small smile. 'Sometimes I feel like it is. But I do know one thing. If we had more people working with these kids, giving them the attention they need, maybe we could learn how to help them.'

There was a faraway look in his eyes, and a deep sadness. And then she knew there was a personal side to this.

'Your brother . . .'

He nodded. 'He got caught up in the gangs. I was in my junior year at high school, trying to pull my grades up so I could get into a university. I wasn't paying any attention to him. I didn't talk, I didn't listen. And then, one year later, a week after his fifteenth birthday . . .' His voice wavered.

Megan put a hand on his arm. 'What happened?' she asked softly.

'One of his pals got his hands on some guns. They tried to rob a jewellery store. The cops arrived, there was a shoot-out . . . my kid brother was killed.'

'I'm so sorry,' Megan whispered, shocked.

He stared past her, at nothing, and she got the feeling he was fighting back tears. She wouldn't have minded if he cried. She would have put her arms around him, comforted him in whatever way she could.

'That's why you became a police officer,' she said.

He nodded. 'I thought it would be a way to make a difference.' Then he looked directly into her eyes. 'I want to be a different kind of cop, Megan. I want to reach these kids. *Before* I have to apprehend them. I don't know how I'm going to do this, but I'll figure out a way. Do you understand?'

'Yes,' Megan said. 'I do.' But even as she said it, she wondered how she could speak with such assurance.

She, who never gave a thought to anyone's needs but her own.

'Do you have problems like this back where you come from?' he asked.

'Of course,' she said. She'd seen TV reports about teenagers who dropped out of school, mindless hooligans who robbed and shoplifted and then drank themselves into oblivion.

'Do they have a better system to deal with these kids?' Frank asked her.

'I don't know,' she said simply. 'I've never really thought about it.' Just saying the words made her suddenly feel so ashamed. 'You were right, you know. I really am a spoiled princess.' She waited for a look of disgust to appear on Frank's face.

But to her amazement, he put his arm around her. 'No, you're not,' he said. 'A spoiled princess wouldn't have listened to me. She wouldn't have cared.'

Megan didn't know what to say. A million thoughts were running through her head and she couldn't make sense of any of them.

'So you really don't want to go to the zoo?' he asked suddenly.

Megan shook her head. 'Do you?'

'Nah, I'm not in the mood any more. You know what

I'd like to do? I'd like to go shopping.'

She looked at him in disbelief. 'You're kidding?'

'I need some clothes, and I never know what's right for me. Could you help me pick out a couple of shirts?'

'I'd love to,' she said, probably with more enthusiasm than the suggestion warranted. 'And you know, I'm pretty good at putting a look together.' Something occurred to her. 'Maybe I could be a stylist!'

'I don't know what that is, but it sounds good,' Frank said. 'Hey, there's a taxi, let's grab it.'

They got into the cab and Frank directed the driver to take them to midtown. Megan was surprised the driver could hear anything, he had his radio turned up so loud. Normally, this would bug her, but her attention was caught by the song playing. It was the same song that they'd heard in the diner.

It Had to Be You.

Was Frank Sinatra trying to tell her something? She glanced at the Frank sitting next to her and felt suddenly that she knew. She knew what the song was telling her.

Frank turned and smiled at her. 'Will you let me take you out to dinner tonight,' he asked.

'Yes!' she said. Too quickly, too happily?

She didn't care.

Chapter Nineteen

Serena wished Jennifer would come back to the suite. It had been hours since they'd separated in the lobby, and Jennifer still hadn't returned. Serena wasn't worried about her, though. She'd probably met a man who was now madly in love with her. It was the kind of thing that happened to Jennifer all the time.

Her thoughts went back to a party Megan had thrown a few months ago. They'd gone together, Serena and Jennifer, because Jennifer didn't want to bring a man.

'I'm in the mood to meet someone new,' she'd told Serena.

Serena wouldn't have minded meeting someone new either. The only difference between them was the fact that Jennifer saw this as a real possibility. For Serena, it was more in the realm of fantasy.

At the party, Serena had greeted Megan, smiled at a

couple of people she vaguely remembered meeting at Megan's before, accepted a glass of wine and looked for a place where she could observe, watch the action, see without being seen. Not that anyone would notice her, even if she stood in the centre of the room.

She did get some very brief attention from a guy she knew slightly. As he passed by, he smiled and said 'Hi.' Serena responded with a 'Hi,' and he moved on. Seconds later, Jennifer appeared at her side.

'You know that guy?' she asked.

Serena nodded. 'He's in one of my classes at uni.'

'Introduce me,' Jennifer demanded.

Serena obliged. The boy was standing alone at that moment, and she led Jennifer to him.

'Mark, this is my friend, Jennifer.'

Jennifer got a 'Hi' from him too, but this time his face lit up as he said it.

'What did you think of that lecture today?' Serena asked.

'It was OK, I guess,' he said, but his eyes were still on Jennifer.

'What are you drinking?' Jennifer asked.

'Punch,' he said. 'Want some?'

'Sure,' Jennifer replied. Then they were gone, and Serena retreated back to her hiding place.

For the rest of the evening, Jennifer and Mark were together, and every time Serena saw them, Jennifer was laughing. Which puzzled Serena, because she didn't think Mark was particularly witty.

She hadn't been jealous, because she wasn't interested in Mark. But she'd envied the ease with which Jennifer had attracted him. And after today's coaching session in the taxi, Serena had a clue as to why he hadn't wanted to talk more with *her*.

'Guys don't want to hear about serious things,' Jennifer had told her. 'Like at Megan's party that time. You started talking to Mark about a college lecture! No one talks about lectures at a party!'

That wasn't the only subject off-limits. Politics, religion, philosophy, your life's goals.

'Then what *do* you talk about?' Serena asked.

'*You* don't talk. Except to ask questions. Keep an element of mystery about yourself. Let *him* talk, and look like you're fascinated by everything he says. Laugh if he says anything remotely amusing. Like this.' And she'd demonstrated for Serena, tossing her head and laughing lightly.

'And touch him,' Jennifer told her. 'Not aggressively. Just lay a hand on his arm, his shoulder. Brush a lock of hair off his forehead.'

So much to remember. Serena was beginning to think her evening with Joe would be more of an ordeal than a pleasure. But she had to believe Jennifer was right. She certainly had more experience with men than Serena had.

Serena had a few friends who were boys. From last night's encounter, she felt pretty sure that Joe could be a friend like that. But this time she wanted more. Joe didn't seem like most guys. He wasn't brash and macho. He was exactly the kind of guy she'd always imagined herself with.

Could it happen for her tonight? Getting off her bed, she tottered over towards the full-length mirror in the bathroom. She'd been walking around in Jennifer's high heels since returning to the suite, and she still hadn't got the hang of it. But she looked pretty good, there was no denying that. She just wished she was more comfortable with the look, with herself. She kept tugging at the neckline of her dress, which didn't actually come up anywhere near her neck, and pulling on the skirt, trying to bring it closer to her knees.

Serena gave up. She might not be at ease with this look, but it was the right kind of look. Now she had to work on what Jennifer called 'the tricks'. She moved closer to the mirror. What was the litany for that look?

Oh right. Duck, tilt . . . what came next?

Look down, slide eyes towards the guy, smile. She tried it a couple of times, but it didn't seem right. Maybe her eyes needed more emphasis.

She went into Jennifer's make-up bag, rummaged around and came up with eyeliner and mascara. Carefully, she added another layer to the goop already on her eyes.

The hotel phone rang, and she picked it up. 'Hello?'

'This is the hotel desk. Miss Kent has a visitor, a Mr Feldman. Shall I send him up to your room?'

Serena swallowed, hard. This was it. 'Yes . . . please.'

She waited by the door, and recalled more of Jennifer's instructions. *Don't act too excited. Be nonchalant, blasé, as if you have dinner dates all the time. Men don't like a girl who seems desperate, they want the girl everyone else wants.*

So when she heard the knock, she didn't respond immediately. She just stood there, holding her breath and waited for a second knock. Then she opened the door.

He looked just as nice as he had the evening before, and he was wearing pretty much the same kind of clothes – baggy jeans, a loose sweater, trainers. His eyes widened when he saw her.

'Wow,' he said. 'You look great.'

Don't get excited. 'Oh, yes,' Serena laughed a weird, high-pitched laugh. 'I was a mess last night, wasn't I.'

'I didn't think so,' he said.

Duck, tilt, down, slide, smile. Joe looked at her oddly, and shifted his weight from one leg to the other.

'Um, these are for you,' he said.

She noticed the flowers and gasped involuntarily. This was the first time ever that a guy had given her flowers. But she mustn't let him think that.

'Thanks,' she said casually, taking the bouquet from him. Then she realised he was still outside the room. 'Oh, come in.'

She wanted to put the flowers in a vase, but maybe that would look like she was making too much of a fuss. So she just tossed the lovely bouquet on the table. Unfortunately, she missed and they landed on the floor. She was about to bend down and pick them up when she remembered how short her skirt was.

'I'll get them later,' she said. Now what? 'Um, would you like a drink? There's a minibar.'

'No . . . thanks,' he said, and glanced at his watch. 'We've got reservations for seven-thirty, so maybe we should take off.'

'OK, I'll get my coat.' As she went to the closet, he glanced around.

'Nice room,' he said.

What would Jennifer say to a remark like that? 'It's OK. All these hotels are pretty much alike, aren't they?'

He laughed. 'Are you kidding? You should see some of the dumps I get stuck in when I'm on tour.'

That surprised her. 'But you sing with important operas!'

'Oh, the big names stay in fancy places,' he told her. 'The rest of us . . . well, let me put it this way – opera singers aren't exactly movie stars.'

A perfect opportunity to do a Jennifer move! Serena tossed her head, laughed brightly and touched his arm.

But Joe just smiled uncertainly. 'Well . . . I guess we should go.'

The restaurant was just down the road, thank goodness. Her shoes weren't made for walking. She was wobbling, and a couple of times she had to grab his arm, not for flirting purposes but to steady herself. He didn't seem to mind, but he was puzzled.

'Those shoes don't look very comfortable,' he remarked.

'They're not,' she said automatically, and then cursed herself. *Never complain*, Jennifer had said. It was a golden rule. 'But it's OK,' she added quickly. 'We have to suffer to be beautiful, you know.' She'd heard Jennifer use that line before.

Joe looked even more puzzled. 'Why bother? Who wants to be in pain?'

She had no answer for that, so she just did another head toss and laughed. She wobbled the rest of the way in silence.

She'd been a little worried when he mentioned reservations. Would this be some kind of super-elegant restaurant where she wouldn't recognise anything on the menu? She was immensely relieved to find them walking into a nice, casual place, where she saw several people eating pizza.

'I know it doesn't look like much,' he said, 'but it's got the best pizza in town, so it's important to have a reservation. On a Saturday night, every restaurant in New York is packed.'

Serena refused to look impressed. 'Oh sure, it's like that in London too. You need a reservation to get in anywhere.'

'I thought you didn't live in London,' he commented as the maître d' showed them to a table.

'Well, no, but I go there all the time,' she lied. 'For parties, dinners. Clubs. There's absolutely no really decent nightlife where I live.' She'd heard Jennifer say

238

that before. Or did it sound like she was complaining? These rules and tricks were complicated. But maybe this was a good time to add a little sparkle to her CV. 'Of course, all the great cities are like this on a Saturday night, aren't they? London, Paris, Rome . . .'

'Do you travel a lot?' he asked.

Uh-oh. What if he started asking her questions about places she'd never been?

'Oh, just the usual places,' she said breezily. 'I'm sure *you*'ve been everywhere. Tell me about your travels.'

He smiled modestly. 'Half the time when I'm on a tour, I don't even know where I am. I see airports, hotel rooms and opera houses. That's about it.' He opened his menu. 'What are you going to have?'

There was a phenomenal listing of pizzas, with varieties and combinations she'd never seen before. *Don't show too much interest in food*, Jennifer had warned her. *If he sees you eat a lot, he'll think you're going to get fat. Men want girls who look and act like models. They never eat.*

'Oh, it doesn't matter, I'm not really into food,' she said.

He actually looked shocked. 'You're kidding!'

Duck, tilt, down, slide, smile. 'Why don't you just order for both of us?'

'OK,' he said, but he didn't seem delighted by the opportunity. 'Is there anything you don't eat?'

Mushrooms, she thought. She absolutely hated mushrooms. But that would make her seem weird . . . 'Oh, I'm fine with anything, I don't really care what I eat.'

Now he was looking at her like she'd just come down from another planet. But he didn't say anything, he just shrugged, and when the waiter came around, he said, 'We'll have the special appetiser plate for two. And a large mushroom pizza. And a bottle of Chianti.' After the waiter left, he turned to Serena.

'This pizza is incredible. They use three kinds of mushrooms, shitake, Portobello and chanterelle.'

She smiled thinly.

'Tell me about your work,' he said. 'What *are* "spiritual motifs" in art? Symbols of religion?'

Serena opened her mouth, then shut it firmly.

No intellectual stuff, no showing off how smart you are.

'Oh, it's sooo boring, you don't want to hear about it and I don't want to talk about it!' What was it Jennifer always said when anyone asked her about university? 'I'm only in at college so I don't have to work. The hours are so much better, I can schedule late classes and sleep till noon every day!'

He had that perplexed look on his face again, and something else she couldn't identify. 'You sleep till noon every day?'

240

She tossed her head and laughed. 'A girl needs her beauty sleep, you know! And when you've been out partying all night . . .'

'I thought you said there was no nightlife in your town.'

Thank heavens, the food arrived and she didn't have to respond. The appetiser plate looked gorgeous – she adored Italian food and this was even nicer than the platter served at Erica's uncle's restaurant. Fried calamari, tomato crostini, prosciutto pinwheels, mozzarella sticks . . .

Joe dug in, heaping food on his plate, and, feeling her stomach growl, Serena was dying to do the same. Instead, she picked up one calamari and nibbled on it. She didn't touch the wine he poured for her – she was such a klutz, what if she spilled it?

She remembered another move Jennifer had told her about. She leaned forward, reached across the table and put her hand on his right arm.

Joe looked at her. 'Do you need something?'

She gave him what she hoped was a mysterious smile. The smile he returned was wary.

'Um, I kind of need that arm to eat,' he said gently.

She removed her hand. Why wasn't Joe responding? Was there something wrong with her face? Maybe her make-up was smeared. Quickly, she reached into her bag and took out the little mirror she'd borrowed from Jennifer's cosmetic case.

Examining herself discreetly, she saw with horror that the extra mascara she'd applied had left a series of tiny but very visible black dots under her eyes. No wonder he wasn't attracted to her!

'Excuse me,' she blurted out, and went off in search of the ladies' room. There, she removed the offending spots, touched up her lipstick and went back to the table. As soon as she sat down, she tried to make up for lost time with a more emphatic duck, tilt, et cetera.

Joe stared at her, a concerned look on his face. 'Are you feeling all right, Serena?'

She tossed her head and laughed.

'Never better!'

The pizza arrived. The mere sight of the mushroom-laden slice that Joe put on her plate made her want to gag. While Joe picked up his slice with his hands and bit into it with gusto, she took a knife and fork and tried to surreptitiously remove enough mushrooms to cut off a tiny bit. Within minutes, she had a little pile of mushrooms on the edge of her plate.

Now he was staring at her again. 'You're not going to eat your mushrooms?'

'Oh, I'm just not very hungry,' Serena said lightly.

This was all going horribly wrong. She looked like a weirdo.

There wasn't much conversation after that. There were things Serena wanted to ask Joe, about his training for the opera, about the roles he'd played and the ones he wanted to play. She wanted to tell him again how beautifully he'd sung the night before. But Jennifer had warned her not to show too much interest, not to act like she was too into him. Which, in Serena's opinion, presented another contradiction – how could she ask him about himself without sounding interested? Maybe it was better to keep her mouth shut and just let him admire her looks.

But clearly, that wasn't going to be enough to keep the evening going. When she refused dessert, he did too, and then he asked for the bill. After he paid, he drummed his fingers on the table and said, 'Well . . .'

She tried to smile seductively, but she was a little light-headed from lack of food. Without a word, Joe helped her put on her coat, and they left the restaurant. When they reached the hotel, Serena remembered Jennifer's final instruction.

'Would you like to come up for a drink? There's cranberry juice in the minibar.'

He shook his head. 'I'm kind of beat,' he said. 'Guess I still have jet lag.'

Serena's heart was heavy. 'Well, thank you for a lovely evening.'

'Sure. Thank *you*,' he said. But there was a flatness to his tone. And suddenly Serena knew the look on his face. It was the expression a child might have when he opens a beautifully wrapped package only to find socks inside.

It was called disappointment. And Serena could totally relate to it.

Chapter Twenty

Slumped in a chair in the lounge of the penthouse suite, Jennifer wondered how much longer she'd have to endure the moronic ramblings of the long-haired greaser sitting across from her. And she wondered what had happened to Jordan.

It was less than two hours ago that she'd entered the suite at the hotel. At the time, she was unbelievably thrilled. Finally, she was getting her big chance, to spend time with a celebrity and see life from the inside of his glamorous world.

She hadn't been in the penthouse long enough on Friday to really admire it. Now, taking a good look around, she thought it was probably exquisite, but she couldn't be sure since it was such an incredible mess.

There were shards of broken glass on the floor and pieces of what might have been an ornate vase strewn among items of clothing she couldn't identify. A chair had been broken, and lay on its side. Remnants of congealed food rested on every surface, along with dirty glasses and a lot of bottles. A magnificent framed mirror over the plush sofa was cracked. And worst of all, there was graffiti all over a wall. She'd read about rock stars wrecking hotel rooms before, but the actual evidence was much worse than the descriptions.

Jordan must have caught her shocked expression. 'We partied hard last night,' he said, with what was unmistakeably a note of pride. Like he expected congratulations for their efforts.

'Didn't housekeeping come today?' she asked.

'I kept the "do not disturb" sign on the door. I ain't gonna deal with the hotel going ballistic, that's Ronnie's job.'

'Who's Ronnie?'

'Our minder. He'll pay 'em off.' He offered her that fabulous lopsided grin she'd seen in photos. 'Ronnie says one of these days the word'll get around and no hotel will take us. I say, that's totally bogus, you get what you want if you spread enough money around. Know what I mean?'

'Oh, absolutely,' Jennifer assured him, as if she was familiar with the concept of spreading money around.

He picked up a cigarette and lit it. Jennifer hated the smell, but she was impressed nonetheless. This hotel had a non-smoking policy, there were signs in every room. Jordan was such a rebel!

'Want something to drink?' he asked.

'Sure. What do you have?'

'I dunno.' He looked around. 'I think there's some champagne.'

'That'll do,' Jennifer said, with the air of someone who drank champagne on a daily basis.

He handed her an open bottle and a glass that didn't look very clean. She was strongly tempted to go into the kitchenette and wash it, but she didn't want to look like she was prissy. This was the rock 'n' roll life, and she'd have to adapt. At least the glass felt like it was real crystal.

Jennifer took a large gulp of champagne and nearly spat it out. Even with her limited experience, she could taste how flat and stale it was.

Jordan yawned.

'I'm gonna take a shower,' he said. 'Wanna join me?'

She wasn't in that much of a rush to get into the lifestyle of a rocker, but she tried to form her response in a way that wouldn't make him think she was horrified by the suggestion.

'No, thanks,' she said airily. 'I've already showered today.'

He shrugged. 'Whatever.' He left her and went into the bedroom.

Alone, she wondered what she was supposed to do now. She pushed some miscellaneous items off the sofa – a T-shirt, an empty shopping bag and a magazine – checked to make sure there weren't any seriously disgusting stains, and sat down. She wanted to pinch herself, she still couldn't believe that she was actually in the same room – well, the same suite – as Jordan Blake. She couldn't wait to tell the others. Megan was always teasing her, saying her celebrity fantasies were totally unrealistic. Wait till she heard about this! She was enormously annoyed not to have her mobile phone with her, or a camera so she could provide real evidence.

She wondered if there was something she could swipe as a souvenir. With two fingers, she picked up the T-shirt she'd swept off the couch. At first, she was delighted to see that it was an official band T-shirt from the tour. But she could have bought one of these at the concert; it wasn't really personal. And the sweat stains under the arms made it less than desirable.

She heard the bedroom door open and she looked up expectantly. But it wasn't Jordan who emerged. A skinny girl in a very revealing top and extremely short shorts, who couldn't have been more than sixteen, ambled out. She didn't seem at all surprised or disturbed to see Jennifer on the couch.

'He's all yours,' she said. She picked up a handbag, threw it over her shoulder and left the suite.

A groupie, Jennifer thought. How sad. There was no way Jordan was going to mistake *her* for one of them.

Finally, Jordan came out of the bedroom. He glanced at Jennifer.

'You still here?'

Jennifer rose and eyed him haughtily, with perfectly arched eyebrows. 'Would you like me to leave?'

'Whatever,' he said. Then she got that great grin. 'No.'

He hunted around the debris covering the coffee table and came up with a remote control. Flopping down on the sofa, he pointed it towards the large flat-screen television on the wall and began hitting buttons.

Jennifer sat back down, but not too close to him. It was important for him to realise she wasn't anything like the girl who'd just left.

She ignored the TV screen, with its rapidly changing images. 'Do you have another concert tonight?' she asked him.

'Huh?' he grunted, still staring at the telly.

She repeated the question and he tore his eyes from the screen for a second. 'Nah, not tonight. We take off in the morning for the next leg of the tour.'

'Where are you going?'

His eyes were back on the screen. 'Dunno.'

'You don't know where you're performing tomorrow night?'

He shrugged. 'Hey, as long as the pilot knows where we're going, I don't care.'

Time for her delighted laugh at his witticism and the light touch on his arm. But he didn't even notice. The phone rang, and he lunged for it.

'Yeah?' There was a pause, and then, 'OK, meet you out front.' He turned to Jennifer. 'Wanna come?'

'Where?' she asked.

'Dunno.'

She began to think Jordan had an extremely limited vocabulary. Well, nobody was perfect, not even a celebrity. Jordan had looks, fame and money, and that was enough to hold her interest.

It took a lot of effort not to act too impressed when they emerged from the hotel. She'd seen lots of limos around New York, but nothing like this. It was the longest vehicle she'd ever seen, and it was white with gold trim. A chauffeur in a uniform opened the door for her. Jordan, however, moved ahead of her and jumped in first. OK, so he didn't have manners, that wasn't the end of the world.

She tried to enter gracefully but it was impossible; given the fact that she had to gently push Jordan to make room for herself. The limo might have been huge, but it was crowded. It was like a train compartment, with two sofa-like seats facing each other. Four people filled up one seat, while Jennifer became the fifth on the other.

She thought she recognised two of the guys as members of Jordan's band, blond and quite fit-looking, but the other three were strangers, and not very attractive. One had greasy hair hanging to his shoulders, the other was bald and covered with tattoos. And there were two girls, both pretty but skanky types.

'Who are you?' one of them asked Jennifer.

Since Jordan didn't appear to be about to introduce her properly, she replied, 'My name's Jennifer. How do you do. And you are—?'

The girls turned out to be Kaylie and Tanya. At least, that was what she thought they said. They giggled as they spoke, so were only semi-coherent. With some additional questioning, she got mumbled responses from the guys, and learned that the two creepy-looking ones were roadies.

'You talk funny,' one of the blond band members said.

So rude, Jennifer thought, but she smiled kindly. 'It's my accent. I'm from England.'

She didn't get any response to that. Of course, these guys probably met people from all over the world; they wouldn't be interested in her just because she was a foreigner.

The car drove around the corner, where she saw a cinema. Whatever it was showing must have been very popular since there was a long line waiting to get in. Looking up at the marquee, Jennifer saw that it was a new documentary movie starring Justin Bieber. That would explain the fact that most of the people in line were twelve-year-old girls.

'Hey, let's start a riot,' one of the band guys said. 'Yo, driver, pull over.'

Jennifer had no idea what he meant, but they'd obviously done this before, because the other band guy and Jordan automatically sprang into action. They opened the limo doors, got out, and Jordan accidentally-on-purpose gently shoved a girl on line.

'Oh, excuse me, I'm very sorry,' he said smoothly, with the first demonstration of courtesy Jennifer had seen from him. The girl turned, and her expression of annoyance changed dramatically when she saw who had just bumped into her.

'Ohmigod, it's Jordan Blake!' she shrieked. And a riot ensued. The line dissolved into a massive onslaught. Girls were waving pieces of paper for autographs, several jumped all over him while others waved their mobiles, trying to get his picture and begging him to be in the photo with them. The ones who couldn't get close to Jordan attacked the other two guys.

Jordan grinned and laughed, signed a few autographs, posed for some photos and kissed a few of them. Then, with effort, they pushed enough girls away to make a path to the limo.

Once they were back inside and the door was closed, the bald roadie yelled 'Go' to the driver.

'Wait!' Jennifer cried out. 'There's a girl on the boot of the car!'

'Tough,' Baldy said. As the car moved, the girl fell off. Jennifer craned her head to see if she'd been hurt, but the limo sped around the corner.

No one else seemed the least bit concerned. The boys were laughing like hyenas, while the two skanky girls raised the volume of their giggles a notch.

Someone pressed something, and a cabinet magically opened. The long-haired band guy took out a bottle of champagne. Jennifer watched in alarm as he shook it. When he popped the cork, a shower of champagne rained through the compartment. A great deal of it landed on Jennifer's trousers and she involuntarily shrieked.

The others seemed to find this hysterically funny, especially since the location of the champagne stain made it look like she'd wet herself. Once the level of laughter began to die down, she spoke with what she hoped had the ring of authority.

'I'll need to go back to the hotel and change,' she announced.

'Aw, c'mon,' Jordan said. 'Don't be a party pooper, it'll dry.'

Of course, his use of the word 'pooper' set off another round of hysteria. They were behaving like primary school infants. Jennifer closed her eyes and tried to stay calm. She had no idea where they were off to now, and she had a sudden fear that it might be a restaurant, or some other upscale place where people would stare at her in her wet jeans.

At least it was dark out now. But when the limo pulled up to a door fronted by a guard and a velvet rope, her heart sank. How could she go inside a club with a stain like this? Maybe she should just make a fast getaway . . .

But then she saw the name of the club, carved discreetly on a little plaque on the wall by the door: Utopia. She drew in her breath. She'd read about this place in countless articles. No photos, though: photography wasn't permitted at Utopia. According to the stories and rumours, this was the wildest, most outrageous night spot in New York, if not the whole of the United States. This was the place where the rich and famous indulged themselves in ways they wouldn't want the rest of the world to know about.

The chauffeur opened the door and they all got out. The bouncer folded his arms across his chest and glared at them until he saw Jordan. Then he relaxed slightly, unclipped the red rope and cocked his head towards the door.

Inside, Jennifer followed the others down a long flight of stairs to a basement level. She needn't have worried about the wet spot on her trousers – it was as dark in here as it was outside. There was music but the place wasn't as noisy as she'd thought it would be. As her eyes adjusted to the dark, she realised that there weren't many people here.

'This place is dead,' Jordan said in a whingeing tone.

'It starts hopping in about an hour,' the bald roadie told him. 'You can have a lap dance while you're waiting.'

That was when Jennifer noticed the barely clad women gyrating on stages spread throughout the room. She tried not to appear shocked, but she'd never seen anything like this in real life.

Jordan took off with Baldy, the two band members disappeared with the two groupies and Jennifer was left with the greasy-haired guy.

It turned out that he was the drummer, and his name was Slick, or maybe Slack, Jennifer wasn't sure. Something like that. He said he was twenty-three years old, but she found that hard to believe. She guessed it was the years of hard living – he told her he'd been playing in bands since he was fifteen, and if every day of his life since then had been like this one, she could understand why his face looked much older.

He flopped down on the couch next to her, and took a swig from his beer. His unfocused eyes turned to her.

'So, you're, like, from where?'

'England,' Jennifer told him for the third time.

'Yeah, right. I been there, I think. Some festival.'

'Glastonbury?'

'I dunno. Maybe. They all look the same, y'know?'

Was he referring to festivals in general or the countries? Probably both, she thought. He didn't seem like the kind of person who was too keenly aware of his surroundings. She looked around the dark, noisy space for any sign of Jordan, but he was nowhere to be seen.

Slick or Slack took another gulp from his bottle. 'Yeah, all the same,' he mumbled. ''Cept Sweden.'

'You like Sweden?' Jennifer asked politely.

'All those blondes. Man, those chicks are hot.' He gave Jennifer an appraising look. 'Like you. You Swedish?'

'I told you, I'm from England,' she said, more impatiently than she intended. 'I'm *English*.'

'Ya might have some Swedish blood,' he said.

She wished Jordan would come back, although she doubted that the rock star would provide much better company. Even so, she forced what she hoped was a sexy smile when she saw him approach. Not too sexy though, as she recalled his invitation into the shower. Flirting was one thing, but she had no intention of following it through. Maybe now that he'd had his lap dance, he wouldn't be feeling too amorous.

'I'm hungry,' he announced. 'Any food around here?'

'Dunno,' the roadie said.

Jordan fixed him with a stony look. 'Find out.'

Slowly, the roadie got up and shuffled off. Jordan slumped down in his chair and spoke.

'Jerks.'

'The roadies?' Jennifer inquired patiently.

'All of 'em. Jerks.'

The people who'd accompanied him here, Jennifer wondered, or everyone in the world? Somehow she didn't think asking would get her any more information.

'You're just hungry,' Jennifer said. 'That's why you're in a bad mood.'

'Who said I was in a bad mood?' he snapped.

She wished he'd show his lopsided grin. He was beginning to seem rather unattractive.

'This place sucks,' he suddenly declared. 'I'm going back to the hotel. Wanna come?'

'What about the others?' she asked.

'Screw 'em,' he said succinctly.

The limousine was waiting for them outside. Jennifer found a spot on the seat that wasn't wet from the spilled champagne. Jordan flopped down across from her.

'Is this what you do every night when you're not performing?' Jennifer asked. 'Cruise around and hang out in clubs?'

He grunted in a way that could have meant yes or no.

'I'm just curious,' Jennifer continued. 'I've always wondered how people who are, you know, well known, live their private lives. Because your life is so public, and people are always watching you. But, of course, you haven't always been famous. Is your life now very different than it was before?'

He stared at her as if she was speaking a foreign language. Then his eyes closed. Was he preparing a profound response to her question? It took a few minutes and the sound of a snore before she realised he was asleep. When they arrived back at the hotel, she had to poke him several times before he opened his eyes. He looked at her blankly.

The chauffeur opened the door, he got out and Jennifer followed. Catching up to him, she said, 'Would you like to go to the restaurant here? It's very nice. But I'd like to go up to my room first and change.'

Again, all she got was a grunt. Apparently, he wasn't interested in the restaurant because he walked in the direction of the lifts. He didn't get very far, though.

A portly man wearing the badge of a hotel employee stopped him. 'Excuse me, Mr Blake, I must speak with you.'

Jordan waved him away. 'No autographs now, man, I'm busy.'

'This isn't about an autograph, Mr Blake. I'm the manager of this hotel, and I would like to speak with you about the condition of your room here at the Palladium.'

The manager was granted the same blank look Jennifer had been receiving from Jordan. But the manager wasn't about to accept it.

He lowered his voice. 'Mr Blake, your suite has been totally trashed, and we need to discuss the situation. Would you please come to my office?'

Jordan behaved as if the man had invited him to jail. He took a step backwards. 'Are you crazy? Don't you know who I am?'

'I am very much aware of who you are, Mr Blake,' the manager said patiently.

'Then bug off,' Jordan said. 'Call my agent.' And he literally pushed the man aside to walk past him.

The manager caught up with him. 'We have been unable to reach your agent, Mr Blake. Now I must insist that you come to my office.'

'Bug off!' Jordan yelled. Jennifer saw his hand ball into a fist. She rushed forward.

'Jordan, calm down,' she began, but he threw a punch. The manager ducked, and it was Jennifer who got knocked to the ground. No one seemed to notice, though. Everyone's attention was on the manager and a security guard who were escorting the rock star away.

'Hey! Are you all right?'

She looked up to see a solid-looking guy a little older

than her, with curly dark hair. He helped her up.

'Thank you,' Jennifer said. 'Thank you very much. I'm fine.'

'Are you sure? You took quite a fall. Did that man push you?' He seemed really concerned.

'It was an accident,' Jennifer assured him. She threw a look at Jordan. 'You must have recognised him.'

'No, I'm not staying in this hotel,' he said, shaking his head.

'I mean, because he's famous! He's Jordan Blake. The rock star?'

He gave her an apologetic smile. 'I'm afraid I don't keep up with rock music. I'm more into classical.'

He had a lovely smile. He wasn't her type – he was a little scruffy and his hair was wild. But he had a cute face. And she really didn't want to spend Saturday night alone in the suite.

She tossed her head and laughed lightly, then noticing him looking a little confused, she put a hand gently on his arm. 'I find it so amazing that one meets people in such interesting ways here in New York.'

'Are you from England?' he asked.

'Why, yes, I am.' She looked down, tilted her head, turned her eyes towards him and smiled. His eyes widened.

'You wouldn't happen to know a girl named Serena Kent, would you?' he asked.

'She's my roommate!' Jennifer exclaimed. Then she felt *her* eyes get bigger. 'Oh! Are you the opera singer she met?'

'Yes.'

'I thought you two were having dinner tonight,' Jennifer said.

'We did. I just brought her back here.'

'Oh, I see.' Jennifer nodded, feeling a little annoyed. Obviously, Serena hadn't followed her instructions very well. 'She really is a sweetheart, you know.'

He nodded awkwardly. 'Well, have a nice evening,' he said stiffly.

Jennifer watched him walk to the door, and sighed. This was not going to be a great night. Serena must be back early because it hadn't worked out with Joe. She was bound to be upset and Jennifer would have to spend the rest of the evening comforting her.

Sure enough, when Jennifer arrived at the suite, Serena was curled up on the sofa in the sitting room looking depressed. At least she wasn't alone. Erica was there too, but looking equally depressed. Jennifer went over and sat down between them.

She turned first to Serena. 'So, I'm guessing it didn't go well.'

'No. Not well at all.'

'Why not? Didn't you follow my instructions?'

'I tried to,' Serena replied. 'I don't think I came over quite right . . .'

Jennifer turned to Erica. 'And Danny?'

'Busy again tonight.'

'Well, if it's any consolation,' Jennifer said, 'my date didn't go well either.'

'You had a date?' Serena asked.

'It wasn't actually a date.' She was about to go into the story when she noticed a light blinking on the phone by the sofa. 'Somebody's got a message.'

Getting up, she crossed the room to the phone. When she pressed the 'message' button. There was a beep, and then a voice.

'This is a message for Jennifer Hawkins. Jennifer, this is Nick Caine. For all I know, you're probably going out tonight and carousing with celebrities. But just in case you're not, I was wondering if you'd like to have dinner with a nobody tonight . . . ?'

Jennifer felt her cheeks heating up and a tingle passed through her. Hugging herself with glee, she noticed her two sad-faced friends staring at her.

She bit her lip. 'Girls, I'd really love to stay here and be sad with you tonight. But, well, it seems I have a date.

A *real* date.'

'Jordan Blake?' Erica asked.

Jennifer shuddered. '*No*, thank you very much. With Nick.'

'Wow! You look so excited,' Serena commented.

Jennifer smiled happily. 'I am. But do you guys mind?' Erica shook her head. 'It's OK, Jennifer. Misery doesn't need that much company.' And Serena nodded in agreement.

'I'm going to change,' Jennifer said. The spilled champagne on her jeans had dried off leaving no stain, and she looked perfectly fine just the way she was. But tonight she wanted to look better than fine.

Chapter Twenty-One

After Jennifer left, Erica got off the couch and went to the window. New York looked so amazing by night. The city that never sleeps. All those lights . . . it was as if each one of them represented a possibility, an exciting option. She could believe what Danny had said about the opportunities that existed in this place, and the more she thought about it she felt shivers travel up and down her spine. He'd made it here, on his own, without an education, with no financial support from his family. Was he unique, or could someone else make it here too? Someone like her . . .

Danny was out there right now, working, fulfilling his dreams. She imagined him in a restaurant, sitting with a couple of high-powered wheeler-dealers, who must have fairly miserable private lives if they demanded a meeting on a Saturday night. But Danny had agreed to meet them, because they needed his advice and he was committed to his work.

Commitment . . . the word made her uncomfortable. Maybe a lack of commitment was *her* problem. She claimed she wanted to be a chef, but what was she doing to achieve that goal? Why would Danny want someone who couldn't move forward?

All these thoughts were disturbing, and she wanted to stop thinking about them. It wouldn't do her any good to sit around and mope. She turned to Serena.

'Want to go out to dinner?'

Serena didn't answer, but the lack of enthusiasm on her face was discouraging.

'Come on, you told me you barely ate anything with Joe, so you must be hungry. It's Saturday night, our last night in New York. We can't waste it sitting around here. Let's get dolled up and go some place cool. A *Babes in Manhattan* kind of place.'

'I'm really not in the mood,' Serena said. 'Honestly, Erica, I just kind of want to be alone. You can go out, I don't need company.'

Erica turned back to the window. She couldn't blame Serena. She knew that feeling; the desire to be alone and not have to make conversation or pretend to be enjoying yourself.

But at the same time, she had no desire to sit by herself in a restaurant. She'd just about resigned herself to an evening of telly and room service when the door to the suite opened. Megan stuck her head in.

'Is everyone decent? Mind if I bring in a guest?'

When no one objected, she opened the door wider. A handsome, broad-shouldered, blond-haired man came in.

'Frank, these are my friends, Serena and Erica. Girls, this is Frank McGuire. *Officer* Frank McGuire. NYPD.'

'You're a police officer?' Erica asked. 'Are you *the* police officer?'

Megan laughed, blushing a little. 'The one and only. We just spent an absolutely lovely day together.'

How quickly things could change, Erica marvelled. Just yesterday Megan had hated this guy. One minute, they were enemies, the next . . . well, from both their expressions she could tell there was some romance blooming.

'How about something to drink?' Megan offered everyone.

'Not for me, thanks,' Serena said quietly. 'It's great to meet you, Frank.' She smiled at everyone before getting up and going into her room.

Megan watched her with concern. 'Is everything OK?'

she whispered to Erica.

'Things didn't work out with her opera singer,' Erica told her. 'She's feeling pretty low.'

'We could ask her to go out to dinner with us tonight,' Frank said, overhearing them.

What a nice guy, Erica thought. She gave Megan a look to signify her approval and Megan smiled in agreement.

'I think she just wants to be alone,' Erica said, smiling at Megan and Frank. 'But it's a kind thought.'

'What are *you* doing tonight?' Megan asked her.

'I guess I'm staying in too,' Erica said. 'Danny has to work. Again.'

'Danny's a big financial advisor,' Megan explained to Frank.

'Well, it's good to know cops aren't the only people who sometimes have to work on Saturday nights,' he said. 'But why don't *you* join us, Erica?'

Erica looked awkwardly at Megan. 'Are you sure? I wouldn't be intruding?'

'Please. We've been alone together all day,' Megan said. 'And . . . I'm hoping we'll have more alone-time after dinner.'

Frank grinned. 'It's a date.'

'Don't worry, I'll make myself scarce after dinner,'

Erica assured them. She went to grab her handbag, and then crossed the sitting room to check on Serena in her bedroom.

'I'm going out with Megan and Frank,' she said. 'Are you sure that's OK?'

'*Go*,' Serena said with a small smile. 'If you stay here, I'll feel obliged to talk to you. And I don't feel like talking to anyone right now. So you'll be doing me a favour if you leave.' She attempted another smile. 'No offence meant, hon.'

'None taken. I totally understand,' Erica said. 'I'll see you later.'

Closing the bedroom door on her friend, she frowned. This weekend was turning into a romantic disaster for some of them. At least Megan had lucked out with Frank.

'Where are we going?' Erica asked Frank as they walked through the lobby.

'One of my favourite restaurants,' he told her. 'A place on the West Side, called Zest.'

'I know that restaurant!' Erica exclaimed. She turned to Megan. 'That's where Danny took me for lunch yesterday.'

'Oh. Then we can go somewhere else,' Frank said.

'There are only about twenty thousand restaurants in New York, I'm sure we can find something.'

'Oh no, I'd love to go back there!' Erica declared. 'I really liked it. There were so many gorgeous things on the menu, I had a hard time choosing.'

Zest was packed, every table seemed to be full, but Frank had called ahead from the taxi and made a reservation. They were shown to a small table in the back, and the maître d' who escorted them gave them menus.

'I'd love to try the lobster roll,' Megan said.

Frank wanted a steak, and Erica decided on the garlic chicken. After all, she wasn't going to be kissing anyone that night.

'Hello, have you decided what you'd like?'

Erica looked up at the waiter. And then she froze. The waiter had the same reaction.

All the colour had drained from Danny's face.

Chapter Twenty-Two

From the bedroom, Serena heard the door to the suite close after Megan, Frank and Erica, and she knew she was alone in the suite. She and Joe had eaten so early, it was only 9.30. The first thing she did was to remove Jennifer's agonisingly uncomfortable stilettos. Then she stripped off the new dress, letting it fall to the floor and not even bothering to hang it up. She put on the baggy tracksuit bottoms, jumper and trainers that she'd worn on the flight to New York, and then she went into the bathroom. It took only a glance in the mirror to know that her carefully applied make-up was now a smudged mess, and she washed off the remains of it.

She performed all these tasks mechanically, like a robot, in a valiant effort to keep her feelings at bay. Then she went back into the sitting room and picked up the remote control.

How ironic that the first image to come up on the screen was the opening credits of *Babes in Manhattan*. The same scene featuring the main characters preceded every episode as the theme music played, and she watched the familiar images of the four girls flash before her eyes. Jane, in a business suit, walking into her office building. Tori, in a ladylike dress, sipping tea in an elegant restaurant. Marina, in a low-cut minidress, dancing on a table with a bottle of champagne in her hand. And finally Kelsey, in jeans, walking hand-in-hand with her boyfriend in Central Park.

The alter egos. Erica related to career-minded Jane, Megan liked Tori, Jennifer was Marina. And Kelsey . . . that was the character she herself supposedly identified with. It was all so bogus. When would *she* ever be walking hand-in-hand with a boy in any park?

It was a rerun from a year ago, a lightly romantic episode about Kelsey and Jason before their big break-up. Sightings of Jason with a beautiful stranger had Kelsey distressed. The story involved some silly misunderstandings, mistaken identities and Kelsey's encounters with obstacles that kept her from realising that Jason wasn't cheating on her. Of course, ultimately everything would work out. Having seen the episode before, Serena knew that.

Some episodes of the show were meant to make viewers feel sad. Serena recalled the one in which Jane's mother died, and when Marina found a lump in her breast. But this wasn't one of them. This was a happy episode.

But Serena was crying. She couldn't help herself. And by the time Kelsey finally learned that the beautiful stranger was an estate agent, that Jason was looking for a bigger flat so he could invite Kelsey to move in with him, that he loved her and all was well, Serena was practically sobbing.

Why was she watching this? She was torturing herself with images of something she'd never have. But the fact was that she could have been watching children's cartoons and still felt the same. Emotional.

This was the real reason she'd wanted to be alone in the suite. She didn't want her friends to hear her, to see her like this. Of course, they would have been kind and compassionate, but that would have made it even worse. Poor, sad, pathetic Serena, loser in love.

Only days earlier Serena had been content with the idea that she would spend her life alone. Then, along came Joe, and her assumptions had been turned upside down. She'd actually entertained the notion that maybe, just maybe, her future wasn't written in stone, that she just might have love in her life.

That connection she'd felt with him on Friday night . . . had she just imagined it? In her subconscious, had she wanted a relationship so desperately that she's fantasised the sense of mutual attraction? Was it not real at all?

But he'd asked her out! Joe must have felt something, or he wouldn't have suggested dinner the next night. And yet it had all gone so terribly, horribly wrong.

She had to stop crying. At any minute, one or more of her friends might return to the suite. She had to pull herself together. Their sympathy would only make her feel worse. She washed her face again and took out her art history book, but that wasn't any help. She kept running into paintings of intertwined lovers.

Maybe she should eat something. But food had no appeal at all, so she succumbed to the time-honoured tradition of what to do when dealing with problems. She went to the kitchenette and made a cup of tea.

She was sipping Earl Grey when the door to the suite opened and Erica came in. It was a good thing that Serena was feeling calmer now, because Erica looked in serious distress. Her face was pale, her eyes were red and she seemed to be shaking.

'Erica? What's wrong?' Serena asked, putting her tea down.

Erica sat down wearily across from her at the little table. 'It's Danny.' Just saying the name sent a tear sliding down her cheek. 'He's been lying to me.'

Serena jumped up and made another cup of tea. Erica accepted it with trembling hands. There was a silence as she took a sip, and Serena waited apprehensively for the story. She had a pretty good idea what she would hear – Erica had been out with Megan and Frank and they had run into Danny with another woman.

'He wasn't working tonight?' she asked tentatively.

Erica put down her cup. 'Oh, he was working all right. He was serving us in a restaurant.'

Serena was confused. 'I don't understand.'

Erica gave a bitter laugh. 'Neither do I. But it seems that my hugely successful tycoon isn't a successful tycoon at all. He's actually a waiter!'

'You're kidding?' Serena got up and put her arms around her friend, listening with disbelief as Erica told her how she, Megan and Frank had gone to the trendy restaurant where Danny had taken her just the day before, and her shock when Danny had appeared at their table to take their order.

'What did he say when he saw you?' Serena said.

'What did he *do*?'

'He did what a waiter does. He said something like, "Do you know what you want to order?"' She gave a wry smile. 'He's obviously a very professional and experienced waiter. He went a little pale, but it wasn't much of a reaction.'

'And what did *you* say?'

'"Garlic chicken, please. With a goat's cheese salad as a starter."' Erica grimaced. 'What else could I say? I wasn't going to question him in the restaurant.' Her elbows were on the table and she rested her chin in the palms of her hands. 'I must have given a pretty decent performance. Megan and Frank didn't have a clue. Oh, Serena, it was a nightmare. He came back with the food, and we didn't even look at each other. And I had to sit there and eat and try to act like everything was normal. Lucky for me, Megan and Frank were so into each other they didn't notice that I wasn't saying much.'

Serena considered the situation. 'You met him on a social network, right?'

Erica nodded. 'Friendspace.'

'And that's where you first learned he was a big shot tycoon?'

Erica nodded again. 'That's not what he put down for his occupation on his info page, of course. He listed himself as an "entrepreneur". It was in our online conversations, when we talked more about ourselves and asked each other questions, that he told me he was a financial advisor specialising in the stock market.'

'So he was trying to impress you,' Serena said.

'I suppose so. I guess he didn't think we'd ever meet.' Erica rose from the table and began pacing the room. 'But we *did* meet. And . . . and I think something was happening between us. Like, maybe we had, I don't know, a future. But he still didn't tell me the truth about himself. He just kept on lying, about his high-powered business and his important connections.'

Serena was on her friend's side, of course, but she wanted to be fair. 'Did he actually lie to you? Maybe he was just embarrassed, Erica. He didn't want to disappoint you.'

Erica stopped pacing. 'Disappoint me? Are you crazy? I was intimidated by him! Hearing how he made it on his own, when I've accepted a future of chopping onions. When I've done nothing to further my career. Yes, I was falling for him, big time, but I felt unworthy of him. And all the time, all the time, he was no better than me.' She sank down on the sofa. 'How could he do this to me? He refused to tell me the truth, and I'm not just talking about his job. He couldn't love me and then lie to me like that.'

'Oh, Erica,' Serena said. 'I'm so sorry.'

'I thought I loved him,' Erica moaned. 'And I don't even know who he is.'

The telephone rang. Erica glared at it balefully and made no move to get it.

'It might be Danny,' Serena said. 'Maybe he wants to apologise?'

Erica shook her head. 'I doubt it. And even if what you say is true, I don't want to hear any apology. I can't forgive him for this.'

The phone was still ringing. It could be Jennifer or Megan with a problem, Serena thought. She went over to the phone and picked it up.

'Hello?'

A receptionist said, 'I have a Mr Feldman in reception, and he would like to see Serena Kent. Shall I send him up?'

Serena couldn't speak. Had she heard correctly?

'Hello?' the receptionist asked. 'Are you there?'

'Um, yes.'

'May I tell Mr Feldman he can come to your room?'

Serena's hand gripped the phone. 'Yes.'

Slowly, she replaced the receiver. Her head was spinning, and she could feel her heart pounding.

'Serena? Who was it?'

She turned to Erica. 'The receptionist at the desk.'

Erica's mouth tightened. 'You didn't tell her she could send Danny up here, did you?'

'No. It's Joe. He's coming up.'

Erica drank the rest of her tea and got to her feet. 'I'll leave you guys alone, then,' she said.

'Don't go, I'm sure he just forgot something,' Serena said as there was a knock on the door.

Erica smiled at her. 'I'll be in my room.'

As Erica moved towards her bedroom, Serena walked slowly to the door. Still in a state of disbelief, she looked through the peephole. Then she opened the door.

'Hello.'

Joe's whole demeanour was softer than before, as he stood awkwardly in front of her.

'Hi.' There was an uncomfortable pause. 'Can we talk?'

Silently, Serena opened the door wider and let him in. Joe stood awkwardly, looking around. His eyes settled on the cups on the table.

'Is that tea?'

'Yes.' She recovered her manners. 'Would you like some?'

'Very much.'

Grateful to have something to do, she went back to

the kitchenette, and returned with a cup for him and a fresh one for herself.

'Lemon? Milk? Sugar?'

'Milk, please.' He smiled. 'I got hooked on milky tea when I was in England.'

She nodded and went back to the kitchen for the milk. She set it on the table and they both sat down. For a moment, they busied themselves putting milk in their teas and stirring. Then there was nothing to do but look at each other.

'You wanted to tell me something?' Serena asked.

He looked down at his tea, and she had the feeling he was putting off what he wanted to say. She took the initiative.

'You don't have to apologise.'

He looked up. 'What?'

These were hard words to say but she had to say them. 'For not being into me. I can deal with it.'

'But I *was* into you.'

She blinked. 'You were?'

'Yesterday, when we met. Only tonight . . . things were different, weren't they?'

'Because I was dressed up? Because I wore a little make-up? Because I wanted to look nice for you?'

He brushed that aside impatiently. 'I didn't care

what you wore.' He took a sip of his tea, and again she suspected he was playing for time. Finally, he found his voice.

'You know, Serena . . . I'm not the world's most secure person when it comes to socialising. I think that's one of the reasons I went into opera. I didn't just want to sing, I wanted to play roles. It was so much easier than being myself. Do you see what I mean?'

'I suppose,' Serena said.

'I wasn't comfortable being myself. And when I was with a girl . . .' he smiled ruefully. 'I didn't think I was very interesting. Or attractive. I didn't know how to make small talk. Or how to flirt.'

Serena raised her eyebrows.

'I was afraid they thought I was too snotty, too intellectual. I wasn't funny, or charming.'

'I thought you were charming,' Serena blurted out.

He smiled again, only this time it was more wistful. 'I know. And it felt so good, like we were really connecting.'

'That's what I thought too,' Serena said. 'Then, why . . . ?'

'I couldn't understand why it was so different tonight, why I didn't feel the same way,' he said. 'And then, after I left you earlier, I ran into your friend.'

'Which friend?'

'I don't remember her name. Blonde hair . . . and she does this.' He shook his head and gave a silly high-pitched chortle.

Serena couldn't help herself, she started laughing. 'Jennifer. That was a pretty good imitation.'

'No better than yours.'

She stopped laughing. 'Excuse me?'

'Well, you were trying to act like her tonight, weren't you?'

Serena didn't know what to say.

'Maybe you look up to her. I imagine she must be pretty popular. Lots of guys like girls like that.'

'No kidding,' she murmured.

'But not *all* guys,' Joe continued. 'Some guys like a girl who's smart, and real, and down to earth. Who says what she thinks, not what she believes someone else wants her to think.' He gazed directly into her eyes. 'Who admits she doesn't like mushrooms.'

Serena's lips twitched into a smile. 'I didn't want to act like I was interested in food . . . Jennifer says that's not attractive.'

'Are you kidding?' Joe exclaimed. 'Food's just about the most attractive thing I can think of! Serena . . . that wasn't you tonight. You were playing Jennifer.' He leaned across the table and took her hand. 'But I didn't want to be with Jennifer. I wanted to be with you, Serena.'

His words echoed in her head, and her heart was full. She wasn't sure if she felt like laughing or crying.

'Would you like a biscuit with your tea?' she asked suddenly. 'Wait, you call them cookies, don't you?' She hurried into the kitchenette and picked up the bag of fancy treats provided by the hotel. She had the bag open as she reached the table and took out a biscuit for herself even before she offered them to him.

'I'm starving,' she said by way of explanation.

'I'm not surprised,' he said. 'Want some real food? We could go back to that restaurant and get another pizza. With no mushrooms.'

Serena got up. 'I should change my clothes.'

'That's totally unnecessary,' Joe said. 'I think you look perfect. You *are* perfect. Just the way you are.'

Chapter Twenty-Three

Jennifer woke up on Sunday morning with a smile on her face. Glancing at the clock, she saw that it was almost eleven. That made sense, since she hadn't gone to bed the night before till almost three. She glanced over at the other bed in the room, but it was empty. She hoped the others weren't already out, doing last minute shopping or sightseeing. She had a story to tell.

Erica was in the sitting room, on the couch in front of the telly with a cup of coffee in her hand. She was dressed but didn't seem to be in any big hurry to go anywhere.

'What are you watching?' Jennifer asked, before yawning loudly.

'Nothing,' Erica said. She pointed the remote at the television and turned it off.

'Want to order a big room-service breakfast?'

'Not really,' Erica said, in the same flat tone.

Jennifer decided against ordering it for herself. She had a lunch date in two hours, so there was no point in eating a big breakfast.

'How was your evening?' Erica asked.

'Brilliant,' Jennifer told her happily. 'Believe it or not, I think I may be into Nick. Isn't that amazingly unreal and totally bizarre?'

Erica smiled. 'Why do you say it's bizarre? He's pretty gorgeous, he's smart, he's nice, he's got a sense of humour . . . what's not to like?'

'It's just that I've always seen myself with someone more, you know, dazzling.'

'Like Jordan Blake?' Erica asked.

Jennifer made a face. 'Actually, I spent some time with Jordan Blake yesterday.'

'Seriously? How? What happened?'

'Long story, I'll tell it when we're all together. It's funny, though. I think maybe celebrities aren't all they're cracked up to be.'

'Perhaps that's why you can now appreciate Nick,' Erica suggested, with a knowing smile.

'Maybe. We had such a fabulous evening! And we didn't do anything glamorous at all. He took me to this pokey little Moroccan restaurant. There were hardly any people there, and none of them looked important.'

'Did you care?'

'No, I didn't! I was having so much fun with Nick, I didn't even want to look for celebrities.'

'Where did you go after?'

'Nowhere! We sat in that restaurant, just drinking wine and talking until they practically threw us out. Then we went for a walk. It was so romantic, the streets were deserted.' She paused. 'He kissed me, Erica.'

Erica laughed lightly. 'Jennifer, you've kissed a lot of boys.'

'I know. But kissing Nick . . . this is going to sound crazy, I know, but he made me feel like I'd never been kissed before.'

'Wow,' Erica said, but there wasn't much warmth in her voice. Jennifer waited for a more enthusiastic response, but there wasn't one forthcoming. She went into the kitchenette to get herself some coffee.

'Where are the others?' Jennifer asked when she came back out.

'Serena's with Joe, he's taken her to some gallery. Megan went out for breakfast with Frank and I don't know where they are now.'

'Wait a minute. You said Serena's with Joe? I thought their date was a disaster!'

'He came over to see her last night. I don't know what happened, I was in the bedroom, but they ended up going out together. I didn't see her this morning, she was out before I got up.'

'And Megan's with – who?'

'Frank, the cop.'

'The cop who was so nasty to her?' Jennifer asked in disbelief.

'Yep. Turns out he's a nice guy.'

'Wow, how did I miss all this?' Jennifer wondered. 'I hope we're sitting together on the flight today so I can catch up on everyone's stories. When are you seeing Danny?'

'I'm not.'

'Why?'

If she'd been surprised to hear that Megan was with the rude police officer, she was stunned to hear about Danny.

'He's a *waiter*?'

Erica frowned. 'Don't say it like that. I know a lot of very nice waiters. But he should have told me the truth about himself.'

'And he's not a rich tycoon,' Jennifer sighed. 'What a disappointment.'

Erica shot her an aggrieved look. 'I don't care if he's

not rich, Jennifer. That's not the point at all. He *lied* to me. That's what's unforgivable.'

Jennifer sat down next to her. 'I'm sorry, hun.'

Erica shrugged. 'It's like the French say, *c'est la vie*. I'll survive.'

'But you really cared about him, didn't you?'

'I thought I loved him,' Erica said softly.

'Then don't you want to know *why* he put on that act?'

Erica shook her head violently. 'There's no excuse for lying.'

'Sure there is,' Jennifer said practically. 'There are all kinds of reasons for telling a lie. He might have a very good one. Aren't you just the least bit curious?'

Erica shrugged.

Jennifer put down her cup. 'Erica Douglas, you listen to me. You say you really care about this guy. Then don't you think you owe him the courtesy of finding out what's going on?'

Erica faced her squarely. 'Jennifer, he hasn't shown up, he hasn't called, he hasn't even tried to apologise or explain. Not that I'd even accept his apology. Why should I go chasing after him for an explanation?'

'Because you've got nothing to lose!' Jennifer declared.

'My pride,' Erica said stubbornly.

Jennifer groaned. 'In a few hours we're getting on a

plane and flying back home. So what if you lose a little pride? You may never see him again. Come on, Erica. What else do you have to do today? Go find him! If you don't, you'll always wonder why he did this. Just do yourself a favour and think about it.'

With that, she went to her room and got dressed. When she came back out, Erica was gone. That was a hopeful sign. Then again, she could have just gone into her room to escape Jennifer's nagging.

Ten minutes later, walking through the lobby, Jennifer could see Nick at the desk, assisting someone. He didn't see her, and she paused for a minute to watch him. He was wearing that same professional smile he'd used on them all when they'd checked in. She hadn't wasted more than a glance at him then. But watching him now, she actually felt a little tingle. Odd, considering he wasn't anyone special. Jennifer shook her head, confused about her feelings. She had to get a grip, Nick wasn't *really* her type, was he? She left the hotel looking forward to a few hours of 'me time'.

One thing Jennifer loved about New York was the plethora of manicure salons. There seemed to be one on every block. This time she splurged on a pedicure too. It was utter bliss, reclining in the chair with her feet soaking in warm sudsy water and reading a magazine.

She flipped through the pages, checking out the photos of every celebrity and reading the gossip. It was funny, though. Now that she'd actually spent time with a real celebrity, they didn't seem quite as fascinating as they used to. And the truth was, she thought Nick was better-looking and more charismatic than pretty much all of them.

Nick was waiting for her impatiently when she returned.

'I thought maybe you'd run into Brad Pitt and blown me out.'

She tossed her head and laughed. 'You don't get rid of me that easy!'

'Well, have you had a good visit?' he asked.

'Fabulous,' Jennifer assured him. 'It's been quite an eye-opener for me.' She glanced at Nick through her eyelashes, but he didn't seem to pick up on her meaning.

'And your friends?' he went on.

'I think they're all very happy. Except maybe for Erica.' Jennifer sighed.

His smile faded slightly. 'What's happened?'

'Well, she found out the guy she's been having an online relationship with has been lying to her. He kind of led her to believe that he was this rich big shot, some sort of Wall Street type. But he turned out to be a waiter.'

Nick seemed concerned. 'He actually lied to her?'

'Not as such, I guess . . . but he certainly didn't tell her the truth!'

'But he's a good guy otherwise, right?' Nick said seriously.

Jennifer shrugged. 'I guess . . . I think she'd fallen for him, if you want to know the truth. She didn't go for him because he was a big shot. She didn't even care what he did for a living. She's angry that he lied to her.'

'Yeah, I guess that's hard to take.'

Nick had an odd look in his eyes that puzzled her. And why would he be so interested in Erica?

'I have to tell you something,' he said suddenly. 'About Danny. The guy Erica's been seeing.'

Jennifer frowned. 'You – how do you know his name?'

Nick sighed. 'He's an old friend of mine. We grew up together, in Brooklyn, went to grade school and high school together. I know all about this online dating . . . When Danny found out Erica was actually coming to New York, he totally freaked out. He knew it was stupid, putting this whole fake ID on Friendspace, but he really wants to get into finance. He was just using the network to try and make some business connections. He didn't expect to fall for her.'

'So Danny's fallen for Erica?' Jennifer asked, her eyes wide.

Nick nodded. 'Even before he met her in person.' He gave her a slightly abashed grin. 'He couldn't believe it when she told him which hotel she was staying in. You know those flowers that were waiting for her when she arrived? They'd been sent to Jordan Blake. I figured he wouldn't miss them, he gets so much of that stuff. I just took the card off, wrote a note and gave them to Erica. It was a favour for Danny.'

'Wow,' Jennifer breathed.

'And he got all his friends at his restaurant to pretend he was a regular customer, just to impress her. And he wanted to treat her to lunch. It was free, you see. Danny can't afford to eat in places like that. He didn't want to lie to her, Jennifer. But he'd already lied on Friendspace, and he was so embarrassed about it, he couldn't tell her the truth.'

Jennifer thought about this. 'Erica says she can't forgive him. But I don't know . . . I think that when you really, truly care for someone, you can always forgive.'

'And from what you say . . . she truly cares for him?' Nick smiled. 'Maybe this relationship can be salvaged?'

Jennifer smiled back. 'And I'm hoping that maybe she's out looking for him now.'

When they finished lunch, Nick asked, 'So, what time's your flight?'

'Seven o'clock, but we're supposed to be at the airport by five. Corona Productions is sending a car to pick us up and take us to the airport.'

That was when it hit her – that she was really leaving, that it could be ages before she'd see Nick again. And maybe this was only a fleeting holiday romance. She'd had those before. There was the ski instructor when she took that vacation in the Alps. The lifeguard at Club Med in Spain. She couldn't even remember their names. Maybe a year from now, she wouldn't remember Nick's.

'What are you thinking about?' Nick asked.

She did her sidelong look and little smile. 'You.' Then, almost involuntarily, she let the mask drop. 'Not seeing you.'

He studied her seriously. 'I hope this doesn't sound too pushy, but . . . you know, this hotel is part of a chain. And we have one in London.'

Jennifer raised an eyebrow. 'And . . .'

'. . . And I've always thought I'd like to live abroad for a while.'

Jennifer looked at him, a smile creeping across her face. 'I've been toying with the idea of moving to London myself. University isn't really for me.'

He grinned. 'That would be – what's the word you English guys are always using? Brilliant.'

Jennifer's smile broadened. Maybe something would come of this, maybe not. But it was fun knowing there were possibilities.

She walked with Nick back to the reception desk, and on their way through the lobby, they saw Erica returning through the main doors. Her woebegone face didn't suggest that things were any better.

'I couldn't find him,' she said miserably. I went to the restaurant, but he isn't working today. And then I went all the way to Brooklyn.'

'Brooklyn? Why?' Jennifer asked.

'He took me to a flat there yesterday. He said it was his cousin's, though now I'm realising that it must have been his. But I couldn't remember how to get there, and I didn't have the address, so I never found it.'

Jennifer put an arm around her, and Erica forced a smile. 'I guess that's that, then. It wasn't meant to be . . . or something like that. I'm going to start packing,' she said sadly, and left to go up to their rooms.

Jennifer watched her friend go, frustrated. There was nothing more Erica could do – they'd be on the plane home soon. It was awful.

But Nick had heard everything. 'I'm calling Danny,' he

told Jennifer, while she waited on the other side of the desk. She watched as Nick got through and started speaking, and she felt hopeful, but when he turned to her, he shook his head.

'I got the answerphone. I left a message.'

Which he might not get before they left, Jennifer thought sadly.

'I guess I'd better go and start packing too,' she said.

'And I'm going to start working on that application for a transfer,' Nick announced. In a lower voice, he added, 'I can't kiss you right here in front of my colleagues. It'll have to wait till I put you in a taxi.'

Jennifer smiled – a real smile, not a tilted-head smile and not accompanied by a head toss. Was that her heart picking up speed? Hearing Nick answering a ringing phone, she practically floated on a cloud all the way to the lift.

Love was all around. OK, maybe not once-in-a-lifetime absolute *love*. But definitely something very like it. She and Nick, Serena and Joe, Megan and Frank. She felt really sad for Erica. But three out of four wasn't bad.

Chapter Twenty-Four

Erica folded a jumper and placed it in the open suitcase sitting on her bed. Then she took it out and refolded it, more neatly this time. Her roommates had finished packing, and both Megan and Jennifer had already dragged their luggage down to the lobby. Erica was taking her time, trying to keep busy for as long as possible. It kept the pain and disappointment at bay. It occupied her mind, and kept her from thinking too much. Or feeling.

As she filled the suitcase, it dawned on her that she wasn't bringing anything back in the way of souvenirs. But that was OK. She didn't really feel like buying anything that would remind her of this weekend and New York City. She supposed she could pick up some things at the airport if she changed her mind. A T-shirt, maybe. And she could buy gifts for her aunt and uncle.

Coffee cups, or key chains, emblazoned with a symbol of New York. Like the Statue of Liberty.

The bedroom door was open, and she could hear the conversation going on between Joe and Serena in the sitting room.

'. . . so if I get the role in Don Giovanni, I'll be coming to London some time just after Christmas.'

'That's perfect,' Serena said. 'I have to do some research at the National Gallery for my thesis, and I could schedule my visit to coincide with yours.'

Erica was happy for Serena, who seemed perfectly fine with the idea of a long-distance relationship. The occasional visit, lots of phone calls, emails, online chat . . . that last thought ignited a memory, but Erica quickly extinguished it. At least Serena knew who she'd be chatting with.

She closed the suitcase, lifted it off the bed and carried it into the sitting room. Now Joe was offering free tickets to the opera, and Serena was promising to act as a personal guide to the art collections in London. It wasn't exactly a romantic conversation, but they were sitting very close on the couch, and Erica thought they needed some time alone.

'I'm going down to the lobby,' she announced.

'I'll see you there,' Serena replied, but her eyes didn't

leave Joe.

In the lobby, Erica found Megan with Frank, standing by two suitcases. Megan had only brought one on her way over.

'I had to run out and buy another suitcase to carry all the things I bought,' she told Erica sheepishly.

'And you're going to have to pay a supplement to check the second bag,' Frank warned her.

Megan shrugged. 'It's worth it. And not just for the clothes.'

'What do you mean?' he asked.

'Well, if I hadn't been running around shopping, I wouldn't have had my wallet stolen. And I wouldn't have met you.'

Frank grinned. 'Yes, I suppose there are some benefits to being a shopaholic. And I can think of another good reason you were deprived of your credit card for at least a short period of time. Imagine, you'd be paying supplements for *two* extra bags, not just one!'

'Oh, stop nagging,' Megan said good-naturedly. 'When you go on holiday, I'll bet you spend more money than you do here.'

'I'm not so sure about that,' Frank countered. 'I can't even remember my last vacation.' He paused. 'You know, I've got two weeks off coming up next month. What's

England like in October?'

'Beautiful,' Megan said. '*I'm* there.'

They moved closer to each other. There were people all around them in the lobby, and Erica hoped sincerely that they weren't about to engage in a public display of affection. She stepped away and turned her head, so their conversation could become a little more personal.

In the lobby, people were coming and going. Excited tourists were just arriving, or looking forward to getting home. Was Erica looking forward to going back? To her pokey room, to her nice but distant aunt and uncle? To a job with no real future? She couldn't really say she'd missed her aunt and uncle, and she doubted they'd been thinking about her.

Serena and Joe appeared, still talking as Joe carried Serena's suitcase to the entrance. And there was Jennifer, coming towards her with a radiant glow on her face.

'Where have you been?' Erica asked.

Jennifer giggled. 'In the cloakroom with Nick.'

Erica rolled her eyes. 'Say no more.' Her tone was jokey, of course, but in the back of her mind she knew she really couldn't stand to hear about any more romantic moments.

And then Nick joined them. He was in his role as

receptionist, and acting very professionally, but Erica didn't miss the gleam in his eye, and the smitten looks he was casting at Jennifer.

'Ready?' he asked Erica and her friends. 'Your car is here.'

And then they were all on the pavement in front of the hotel, by the van labelled Corona Productions. The driver and a bellhop began loading the luggage in the boot. Erica saw Serena and Joe talking softly, and she suspected they weren't discussing art or opera. Frank and Megan were gazing deeply into each other's eyes. And even Nick discarded his professionalism for a moment to give Jennifer one last kiss.

Erica climbed into the van first. She wanted a place by a window, so she could pretend to be looking at the view. She knew there would be a lot of happy chatter going on among the other three, and she wouldn't be able to join in. And as the van took off, she kept her face pressed to the window. They got on a highway, and she watched New York disappear. Then, with nothing much to look at, she closed her eyes, leaned back in her seat and tried to sleep.

She couldn't, of course. All she could see was Danny's smile, that sensitive face, the eyes so blue she could drown in them. And hear his voice. All those lovely little lies.

And then they were at JFK, with all the hustle and bustle of a major airport, only more so. There was the confusion of locating the right terminal, fumbling in bags for passports and tickets, then finding the check-in desk.

Jennifer gathered all their tickets and went up to the desk. In triumph, she called over her shoulder to the others.

'We've got seats together this time!'

A cheer went up from Megan and Serena. Erica smiled too, but inside she was moaning. They'd be sharing their stories all the way back to the UK. Erica wouldn't be able to sleep. And she wouldn't be able to contribute.

Once they'd handed over their bags and secured their boarding passes, it was off to the security area, and they joined the queue to go through the inspection. That was when the woman from Corona Productions, Heather Something, caught up with them.

'Girls, girls, we need a photo to show your departure,' she cried out. 'Now, I want huge smiles, excited smiles. I want you to look like you just had the most fabulous weekend of your entire lives.'

It was easy for Jennifer, Serena and Megan. Erica bared her teeth and hoped it resembled a smile.

'Look over here,' the woman screeched. 'You, the one with the red hair, look at the camera!'

But Erica's eyes were focussed elsewhere. Just outside the rope that separated the passengers from everyone else stood Danny.

He was searching the crowd, but he hadn't spotted Erica yet. The line of people inched forward. She stared at him and willed him to see her. And finally, he did. With the noise and the distance, he couldn't speak and be heard. Erica didn't know how to lip read, but she understood when his mouth formed the word, 'please'.

'I'll be right back,' Erica said, and she ducked under the rope. She was aware of a guard frowning as he watched her walk purposefully over to the young man, but she ignored him.

'Hello,' Danny said.

She wasn't going to waste what little time they had on pleasantries. 'You lied.'

He nodded. 'I never thought I'd actually meet you.'

'But you did,' Erica said. 'And you kept right on lying.'

'It wasn't completely false, what you thought about me,' he said. 'The person you thought I was . . . he's the person I want to be.'

'I don't understand.'

'You see . . .' Danny took a deep breath. 'What I told you, about my father, about how I want to help people

302

invest wisely and not make stupid decisions, that's all true. I'm just not doing it yet.'

'Then why did you pretend? Why didn't you tell me?'

'Because . . . because I was ashamed. I *am* ashamed. You liked this guy you met on Friendspace, this successful go-getter, this junior tycoon. I didn't want you to know what a screw-up I really am.'

He fell silent, and Erica didn't know what to say. Should she tell him that his 'success' wasn't the only attractive thing about him on Friendspace? And then accept his apology, shake hands and return to her friends? Her mind was racing and going nowhere.

'I wanted to make it on my own, that was my plan,' Danny said. 'But I didn't.' He smiled wryly. 'It seems no one wants advice from a guy who doesn't have a degree to back him up. It's just like your situation. You told me you can't get a job in another restaurant without some kind of qualification.'

Erica nodded. She understood how it worked all right. 'What are you going to do?' she asked him.

'I'm going back to school,' he said. 'I'll get a scholarship or a student loan to pay the tuition. I'll go on working in the restaurant to support myself. And somehow, someday, I'll get there. I'll be that person you met on Friendspace.'

'That . . . that sounds like a good idea,' Erica said carefully.

He took another deep breath. 'There's one thing I didn't lie about, Erica. I really, really like you. And I think maybe we could be even closer.'

And then, in a flash, all the hurt and the anger and the sense of betrayal subsided. Her words came out effortlessly.

'Yes. I think so too.'

'Then stay with me, Erica.'

'What?'

'Stay with me here in New York. Don't go back to England. You're not happy with your life there, you told me that. You can go to a cookery school here. And you can work in the kitchen at Zest. And you won't have to chop onions. Well, not all the time. I talked to the chef, I told him about you. You can learn from him.'

This was crazy, it was utterly insane. To make a decision like that, right here and now. It was too sudden, too drastic. She couldn't just give up the life she knew, with the snap of two fingers. She needed time to think . . .

To think about what, she asked herself? Her lonely room, her boring job . . . a life where watching a television show was the highlight of her week?

She turned to see her three mates, all watching her. Had they guessed what he'd just asked? Heather and her photographer were watching too. The queue had moved, the girls were now closer to the security check, but there was still time for her to join them before they passed through.

Just enough time to say goodbye.

She turned back to Danny, he opened his arms, and she fell into them.

'Yes,' she whispered. That was the only word she could get out before she was silenced by his kiss.

She could hear the Corona woman yelling to the photographer. 'Get that! It's perfect!'

Erica smiled. That's what this was to them – a perfect *Babes in Manhattan* moment. A New York weekend romance. What they couldn't know was that they were capturing the moment when Erica Douglas decided not to go back.

But to stay in Manhattan and start the next chapter of her life . . .

TICKET
TO
LOVE

Marilyn Kaye answers our questions!

What was the inspiration behind Ticket To Love?
Many of the best times I've ever had took place on vacations with girlfriends. I've never taken a trip quite like the one described in Ticket to Love, but it's the kind of adventure I would love to have.

What is it about Paris that made you move there?
Cheese, wine, and romance!

What is your favourite song and why?
'Imagine' by John Lennon -- because it expresses the most beautiful hope for a better world.

If you could invite 5 people to dinner, who would you invite?
1. Barack Obama -- because he's so intelligent
2. Cleopatra -- powerful women are fascinating
3. The Dalai Lama -- because he's kind and generous and he has a wonderful laugh
4. William Shakespeare -- because he could give me some tips on plotting and character development
5. Lady Gaga -- because she seems like she'd be great fun.

What is your favourite book?
Pride and Prejudice by Jane Austen -- I like stories that blend romance with humour.

How do you get your ideas?
Are they ever based on real life experiences?
Ideas just seem to pop into my head, and I honestly don't know where they come from. Sometimes I do draw on real experiences, but I have to use a lot of imagination to make them interesting enough to read about.

Where is your favourite place to write?
I can write just about anywhere, but I particularly like sitting at my desk facing a window that looks out over Paris rooftops. Sometimes I like to write in cafes, too.

If you weren't a writer, what career do you think you would have?
That's a hard one, because I can't really imagine doing anything else. But I love fashion, so maybe I'd enjoy being a designer.

Do you have any top tips for aspiring young writers today?
The best advice I can give is to keep a private journal and try to write in it everyday. Let you mind wander, jot down your thoughts, your ideas, your fantasies -- this is how stories begin.

The DUFF

Seventeen-year-old Bianca Piper is smart, cynical, loyal - and well aware that she's not the hot one in her group of friends. But when high-school jock and all round moron Wesley Rush tells her she's a DUFF - a Designated, Ugly Fat Friend - Bianca does not see the funny side.

She may not be a beauty but she'd never stoop so low as to go anywhere near the likes of Wesley ... Or would she? Bianca is about to find out that attraction defies looks and that sometimes your sworn enemies can become your best friends...

Funny, thoughtful and written by the author when she was only 17, this novel will speak to every teenage girl who has ever thought they were a Duff.

April 2012

www.hodderchildrens.co.uk

Hodder Children's Books

EVERYTHING STARTS RIGHT HERE RIGHT NOW

MOMENTUM

SACI LLOYD

London, the near future. Energy wars are flaring across the globe - oil prices have gone crazy, regular power cuts are a daily occurrence. The cruel Kossak soldiers prowl the streets, keeping the Outsiders - the poor, the disenfranchised - in check. Hunter is a Citizen: one of the privileged of society, but with his passion for free running and his rebel friend Leo he cannot help but be fascinated by the Outsiders. So when he meets Outsider Uma, he is quickly drawn into their world - and into an electrifying and dangerous race to protect everything they hold dear.

A hugely exciting dystopian thriller from the immensely talented Costa-shortlisted author of The Carbon Diaries, Saci Lloyd.

'From its breathtaking opening ... an action-packed thriller with a warm heart' – The Gu

Also available as an ebook

www.hodderchildrens.co.uk

Join our Review Crew!

www.hachettechildrens.co.uk/reviewcrew

Would you like to help us make our books even better?

Your opinions really matter to us! We've put together some simple questions to help us make our books better for you. Fill in this form (or a photocopy of it) and send it back to us, or go to www.hachettechildrens.co.uk/reviewcrew to complete the same form online.

Would you recommend this book to anyone else?

☐ Yes ☐ No

If yes, why would you recommend it?

What book are you planning to read next?

Which other authors do you enjoy reading?

Would you like to join our 'Review Crew'?

☐ Yes ☐ No

Members of our 'Review Crew' receive copies of our books in manuscript form with a simple form to complete to tell us what they thought. We'd also like feedback from our 'Review Crew' about cover designs.

How old are you?

☐ 5-6　☐ 7-8　☐ 9-11　☐ 12-14　☐ 15+

Name _____

Address _____

_____

Email address _____

Please get a parent or guardian to sign this form for you if you are under 12 yrs old

Signature of parent/guardian _____

Name in block capitals _____

Date _____

We will only use your address to send you review manuscripts and guarantee not to send any further marketing or adverts, or pass your address on to any other company. However, if you would like to receive appropriate newsletters full of authors news, sneak peeks, competitions and special offers from Hodder Children's Books and associated Hachette Children's Division companies please tick the box and ensure you supply an email address above.

Please send this form to:
Review Crew, Hachette Children's Books, 338 Euston Road,
London NW1 3BH or alternatively go to
www.hachettechildrens.co.uk/reviewcrew
and complete your form online.

TICKET TO LOVE /2011